TRUTH IS
A BRIGHT STAR

TRUTH IS A
BRIGHT STAR

JOAN PRICE

TRICYCLE PRESS
Berkeley, California

To my father and mother

Copyright ©1982 by Joan Price

Tricycle Press
P.O. Box 7123
Berkeley, California 94707

Cover painting by Enrique Moreiro
Book decorations by Lilian Cram
Typography by HMS Typography, Inc.

The text of this book is set in Times and Benguiat.

The Library of Congress has catalogued an earlier edition as follows:

Price. Joan.
   Truth is a bright star.
   Bibliography
   Summary: Understanding and finally friendship develop between a twelve-year-old Hopi Indian boy and the fur trapper who bought him from Spanish soldiers in 1832.
      1. Hopi Indians—Juvenile fiction.
[1. Hopi Indians—Fiction. 2. Indians of North America—Fiction.
3. Slavery—Fiction.   4. New Mexico—History—To 1848—Fiction.]
I. Title.
PZ7.P9304Tr   [Fic]   82-1345
ISBN   0-89087-333-X (pbk.)   AACR2

First published by Celestial Arts, 1982
First Tricycle Press printing, 1997
Revised edition, 2001
ISBN 1-58246-055-8

Printed in Canada

1 2 3 4 5 6 — 06 05 04 03 02 01

FOREWORD

The Hopi call themselves the "People of Peace." Their ancestors came to the land we call the United States across a land bridge from Asia over thirty thousand years ago; they may even have been the continent's first settlers. The Hopi village of Oraibi in Northern Arizona is the oldest continually inhabited village in the U.S. Oraibi sits perched atop one of three rocky plateaus rising six hundred feet above the vast desert floor. Because of their level tops, these plateaus are called mesas, from the Spanish word for table.

Long ago, the Hopi lived at the base of the mesas on the desert prairie near their corn and melon fields. Then, in the mid-1700s, when raiders such as the Spanish and Navajo regularly plundered Hopi villages, the Hopi took refuge on the mesa tops. Hopi men walked more than ten miles a day down steep paths carved into the cliffsides to tend their crops on the desert floor, while women gathered water from the small springs at the base of the mesas.

The Hopi have a deeply spiritual view of the world. They believe their lives are integrally woven in a universal plan of creation which is revealed every year through the cycle of ceremonies. These religious ceremonies are meant to ensure harmony in the universe. One of the ceremonies, called Sóyal, takes place during the winter solstice and celebrates the second phase of Creation at the very beginnings of life on earth. It is also referred to as Sóyalangwul, which means, "establishing life anew for all the world." During Sóyal's secret ceremonies, in which only the initiated participate, the Hopis send prayers to the Creator asking for rain for their crops and harmony to all creatures.

In December, 1832, as the Hopi prepared for the sacred Sóyal ceremony, a group of Spanish soldiers stormed the village of Oraibi. Loma's story begins on that December day, just before the winter solstice.

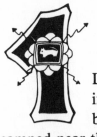 Loma and his dog stood on the mesa top look-
ing down. Through the evening shadows the
boy watched a group of Spanish soldiers
camped near the spring at the mesa bottom. It was December, 1832, four days before the Hopi Indian Sóyal ceremony.

In his eleven years, Loma had never seen a white man.
But he had heard his grandfather and some of the older men
of the village tell stories about how the Spaniards used to
loot Hopi villages, steal corn from their fields and kill any
man who tried to stop them. He remembered the story his
grandfather had told him about the first time the Spanish
soldiers had come to the land of the Hopi.

"Our people," his grandfather had said, "were happy to
see their white brother. They drew a line of sacred corn meal
across the trail to welcome them. The line meant they would
live side by side, join together in truth and share the land.
But the Spaniards did not want to live in brotherhood. They
attacked the villages and made our people submit to their
rule."

1

"Their rule, Grandfather?"

The old man had nodded. "The Spanish chief from New Mexico wanted our people to follow their laws. His soldiers brought priests and forced our people to join a foreign religion. If a Hopi man refused, he was beaten or killed. Soon the crops of our people failed, and they knew that the religion of the Spaniard was not right for them. The Hopi accepted their rule, but refused to practice the foreign religion."

"What did the Spanish chief do, Grandfather?"

"The Spaniards wanted gold and silver. Our land held none. They left our mesa to search for treasure."

"I have heard that the Spanish soldiers war against the Navajo," Loma said.

"Yes," the old man had answered, "they are always at war with each other. The Navajo steal their horses and sheep. They raid the Spaniards, and the Spaniards raid them."

Sharp laughs sounding from below echoed off the cliff walls and soared up to the mesa top. The dog growled. Loma knelt beside him, worked his hands gently over the long tan hair.

The boy listened and waited. Loma wondered why the Spanish soldiers were here now. He would have liked to ask his father, but all the Hopi men were in the underground kivas making prayer sticks for Sóyal, the ceremony dedicated to give aid and direction and strength to budding life.

The low growl rumbled again in the dog's throat.

"You are right," he said to the dog. "There is something bad in the soldiers' laughter. The sounds they make are like dark clouds hiding the sun on a happy day."

2

Loma turned to see his mother and the other village women filing out of their stone houses carrying piki bread and corn. Quietly, they moved through the village streets to the steep path leading down the mesa. As the women passed him, his mother smiled. He wanted to talk to her, to ask why they were taking food to the Spanish soldiers camped with their horses at the Hopi spring. But the silence of the women was too heavy for his words right now.

Slowly, they moved down the dirt path toward the Spaniards. Loma watched and waited. The dog growled and the hair on his back bristled. More laughter was heard, louder than before. Foreign words, strange to Loma's ears, followed the Hopi women as they returned up the worn path empty-handed. Loma turned away from the mesa edge and, with the growling dog at his heels, followed his mother to their home.

The boy was glad to be inside the warm house. He spread his sleeping blanket on the floor and sat down. The dog snuggled up close to him. Loma looked at his mother, his dark eyes wide with curiosity. She spread a blanket on the floor and sat down cross-legged near him, ready to answer his questions.

"Mother, why do our people feed the Spaniards?"

She looked at him. "Because they are hungry. It is the duty of every man to feed his brother when he is hungry."

"The Spanish soldiers are our brothers?"

"It is the law of Creation that all of life is our brother; the living stones, the breathing mountains, the plants, the animals and mankind. Whatever form it takes, life is our brother. We are all part of the one great life that cannot be separated."

"But, Mother. The Spaniards steal and kill. They do wrong."

"Have you seen this?"

Loma shook his head. "But Grandfather has seen it. You have heard the stories."

"Yes, my son. Long ago the Spaniards looted our villages and killed our people. That is in the past. We are Hopi, the People of Peace. It is our duty to live in harmony with all things. The Spaniards must be forgiven for what their grandfathers did to us."

Loma frowned. "I do not like the sound of their laughter."

Worry showed on his mother's face for only an instant. Quietly she said, "Is my son so wise that he can judge what is in a man's heart by the sound of his laughter?"

Loma looked directly into her dark eyes. They reminded him of still pools of water. "My father's laughter is a song upon the wind. It brings joy."

The woman smiled. Without a word she drew a blanket up over her son and his dog. Her hand touched his forehead. It was time for sleep.

While Loma slept he dreamed of the Spaniards and tossed and turned on the blanket; then finally he stopped dreaming and was quiet.

Shortly after sunrise Loma was awakened by a shrill blast from a horn. It startled him to his feet. He wrapped the blanket around his shivering body and raced to the window in time to see the Spanish soldiers ride their horses into the village plaza. Then he saw the soldiers jumping off their horses and running through the dusty village streets. It seemed they were trying to catch children!

The Spaniards fired their guns at the Hopi men who ran out of the underground kivas. Loma gasped when he saw his uncle shot while he was trying to protect his son. His stomach tightened as he watched the soldiers scalp the Hopis they killed.

Suddenly the door to his own house flew open and a soldier rushed in. The dog sprang at the soldiers's neck, then dropped limp to the dirt floor. The soldier wiped the blood from the knife on his pant leg before slipping it again beneath his belt. In that instant Loma's mother ran between the Spaniard and her son.

The soldier shoved her roughly against the stone wall and laughed. As the man came toward him, Loma regained his senses. He ducked, wiggled out of the soldier's grasp and ran out the door.

Once in the street the terrifying confusion of gun shots, screams and shouting sounded in his ears. He ran faster. Halfway down the dusty street a soldier grabbed him. At the same time Loma's father rushed out of the kiva and threw a blanket around the boy to protect him. While the two men were fighting for possession of the boy, a second Spaniard came up and fired his gun. Loma and his father fell to the ground. The Spaniard who had fired jerked off the blanket. Blood ran from Loma's father's arm. The two soldiers seized Loma up between them and dragged him to their horses.

Some of the Hopi children were scurrying to the flat rooftops of the houses, but soldiers followed. Above the dust and confusion came the voice of the Oraibi village chief. Even as he spoke, the people were grouping together and rushing at the Spaniards with heavy rocks and sticks. The Spaniards fired at them, but were unable to reload their guns fast enough to cope with the furious villagers. Quickly the soldiers mounted their horses and fled from Oraibi, taking with them fourteen Hopi children and Butterfly Girl, the young wife of Wickvaya, a Hopi youth. Only two Spaniards stayed behind to be buried by the village people.

The Spanish soldiers galloped across the tiny corn fields driving the Hopi sheep before them. Then, with the fourteen captured children and Butterfly Girl, they headed away from the People of Peace toward Santa Fe, New Mexico.

Loma was held stomach down across the saddle in front of a Spanish soldier. He fought; he kicked his bare feet and pounded on the soldier's leg with both arms. When he saw that his struggle was useless, he lay still. Then, unexpectedly he turned his head and sank his teeth into the soldier's leg. The Spaniard howled, jerked the horse to a stop and brought his hand down swiftly on the back of Loma's neck.

The boy's eyes opened wide, then closed into unconsciousness. Later when Loma awakened, he was sitting, hands tied, behind the soldier. Around his waist was tied a stiff rope joining him to the Spaniard. Frightened, he looked cautiously out of the corner of his eye at his friends. Some of them were tied as he was behind the soldiers. Others were held in front of the soldiers. Butterfly Girl was tied to a horse by herself. As they traveled over the vast Arizona desert the children said nothing, but their eyes were anxious, wondering.

On and on they rode through the painted desert. Loma turned to look at the land they were leaving behind. Within his heart the call of his people came on the feathers of eagles, joining forces with him, giving him strength. There was no sound. There was only the knowing.

As the shadows lengthened, the Hopi villages perched on top of the distant mesas were lost to sight. The setting sun cast a red glow outlining the rugged plateaus against the sky. Slowly the sun slid behind the distant mesas to put the day to rest and the homes of the Hopi children could be seen no more.

During the night the children and Butterfly Girl were left tied in a circle on the ground. The soldiers butchered four sheep, then they ate mutton and what was left of the piki bread given to them by the Hopi women. They offered the children a little food, but no water, keeping what they had left for themselves. Shortly after dark, a young Spaniard slipped away from the group of sleeping soldiers and came with his canteen to the children. No words were spoken as he tipped the canteen to each thirsty mouth, giving each his share of the water.

Loma gazed intently into the Spaniard's eyes. In them he saw sadness and he knew the young soldier was crying in his heart for what had been done. The edges of Loma's lips lifted in a smile. He did not know why, perhaps to help wipe some of his own bitterness away. The young soldier turned away and hurried back to the others.

When the soldier was out of hearing distance Loma turned to Butterfly Girl. "Why do you think the Spaniards have captured us?" he asked.

"I have heard," she whispered, "that the Spaniards capture Indians to sell them as slaves in Santa Fe. Wickvaya has told me of Navajo children stolen from their families and sold for slaves."

Loma scooted over closer to her. "But we are not Navajos," he whispered. "We do not steal the Spaniard's horses."

Butterfly Girl nodded. "What you say is true. I do not know the answer. What I tell you is what my husband told to me."

Loma rubbed his feet against each other to warm them. "Butterfly Girl," he questioned in a whisper, "What is a slave?"

In a voice so low that Loma could hardly hear, Butterfly Girl explained. "Our people do their own running. We run from the mesa top to our fields below the mesa each day of the sun and the rain. The horse does the Spaniard's running for him. The horse is the Spaniard's slave."

Loma frowned beneath the bang of his straight-cut hair. "A slave is one who does another man's work?"

"Yes. That is what a slave is for."

Loma cupped his chin in both hands. His thoughts whirled like the dust in the wind. His father had always said, "A man must do his own share. Work is good for the soul."

Loma sat there thinking, Butterfly Girl covered his bare feet with the edge of her skirt. It was winter. In the morning, frost would cover the ground. Soon Loma lay back and closed his eyes to the world around him. Thoughts of his little tan dog, whose spirit had been released from his body, came to him. The boy could feel the little dog's spirit with him now, free, as the wind was free. But knowing the dog's spirit was free seemed empty to him. Loma needed more. He needed to hold his dog close and share the warmth of his friendship.

Day after day the band of soldiers and the captured children traveled over the vast desert that stretched out for miles in all directions. The sheep that the soldiers had run off from the Hopi people dropped back unable to keep up with the horses no matter how hard the Spaniards tried to herd them along. After a week of traveling the mutton was gone. The children ate roots from the desert plants to stay alive.

The insides of Loma's legs had raw sores from rubbing against the saddle. But he said nothing for he knew the other children must also have sores. Beneath his brown skin big bruises shone purple from the tight ropes around his hands and waist. Loma watched the other children. The pain in their eyes told him it was the same for them. No one cried out. They rode in silence on and on toward Santa Fe.

The soldiers grew tired and spoke to each other sharply. Loma listened to the words. He listened to the tones. Then to take his mind off the aching muscles, he placed the words on his tongue and moved them around. The young Spaniard who had offered water to the children watched the Hopi boy. Seeing how intently Loma listened, he decided to trade the Hopi girl he was carrying on his horse, for the boy. The soldier Loma rode behind listened to the younger soldier's proposition. He thought that the girl weighed less than the boy. Besides, the boy had done everything he could think of to make the trip miserable for the soldier. He had leaned sideways, off balance, forcing the soldier to stop his horse and rest. The boy had refused to get on the horse in the mornings or to get off of him at night. The soldier was forced to drag him off the horse and carry him to the group of children where he was to sleep. When the young Spaniard offered to trade the girl for Loma, the soldier gratefully agreed.

For the rest of the trip the young Spaniard rode behind the group of soldiers so he would not be seen teaching Loma the Spanish language. The soldier pointed to the trees, to the ground, to the clouds and the sky. Each time he pointed, he named the object in Spanish. At first Loma said nothing, but he formed the words carefully on his tongue and held them there. Later he whispered the words, but never did he talk to the soldier. The young Spaniard knew that the boy wanted to learn whether he talked or not. And teaching the boy gave the soldier something to do with his time on the long trip to Santa Fe.

The snow came when they were a few days outside of Santa Fe. The children and Butterfly Girl huddled close together for warmth. They had no blankets. Most of the children had bare feet, for they had been dragged out of their beds the morning the Spaniards invaded the village of Oraibi. During the day as they rode on the horses behind the soldiers their naked feet dangled in the chill air. Some children had frostbite and after a long day of riding, they were not able to stand without help.

The young soldier offered Loma his socks.

Loma looked longingly at the dirty socks, then shook his head. If the other children must suffer from the cold he would be no different.

The soldier shrugged his shoulders, pulled on the dirty socks, then the worn boots, and mounted on the saddle in front of Loma. After a few miles of riding in the cold the soldier motioned Loma to tuck his feet between the stirrup leathers and the horse. Loma was not pleased with the idea of touching a Spaniard. But after a few hours of bitter cold biting into his bare feet, he shyly moved both legs forward until his feet were between the Spaniard's legs and the horse. Soon the body warmth of the horse brought the feeling back to his numb toes. He noticed the other children had also pressed their bare feet against the horses' sides.

On the last day of the long trip howling winds sprang up, racing across the face of the earth. Loma shivered. The cold wind drove snow from the sky and the ground. It was a loud wind sweeping down from the mountains. All day the sun slept behind heavy clouds. Day and night had blended into one. It seemed to Loma they were riding through the world somewhere outside of time.

Suddenly, unexpected voices rose through the darkness. Loma listened. Soon he was able to distinguish dull lights and a vague outline of buildings. The young soldier stood up in the stirrups. "Santa Fe!" he shouted.

Loma felt his heart skip. He forgot the stinging cold. He forgot the ache in his body. Afraid to see Santa Fe, he turned in to himself and soon a vision of his mother and father sitting in the stone house on the high mesa top came to him. In silent meditation they sent prayers to the four directions. And Loma lifted his heart to them and heard his father's voice singing in the night.

The horses stopped and the soldiers dismounted. Loma turned his eyes upward to the heavens. Now that they were in Santa Fe the young soldier grew impatient. "Dismount!" he ordered.

The boy looked down. Slowly he slid from the horse. When his feet touched the ground, sharp pains shot up his legs as if he were standing on hot pieces of broken pottery. He stood quietly, saying nothing, looking at nothing.

"Hurry. Get inside," the soldier said impatiently. "I do not wish to linger here, I wish to celebrate!"

Loma looked at him, puzzled. The man who had tried to be his friend was not the same man now. Loma did not understand all of the spoken words, but he understood the soldier's tone which had changed from one of kindness to irritability. He followed the other Hopi children inside the dimly lighted room.

They were herded into a smaller room to the rear. It was a cold room of adobe brick with one barred window and a thick wooden door. When all the children were inside the small enclosure there was scarcely room to turn around.

"Untie them!" commanded the leader. "Alfredo," he said to a man in uniform who stood waiting with a set of keys in his hand, "bring the captives food and water. We will come for them in the morning."

Alfredo nodded and bolted the door.

Later the door opened and Alfredo entered with a pot of cold pepper stew and one wooden bowl. He set them on the floor and hurried out of the small room bolting the door behind them.

The children passed the bowl around until the pepper stew was gone. They talked little. Words were not needed. Finally they lay down on the dirt floor squeezing into the small space by having the younger ones lie on top of the older ones. The children were tired, almost too tired to care. But they were too afraid not to care and they slept restlessly all night.

One by one the children were led out of the small adobe room into the larger room in the front of the building. The place was filled with Spanish soldiers and ranchers. To one side of the crowd stood a large man dressed in buckskin and moccasins. His hair and beard, unlike those of the others, were reddish-blond and his hard blue eyes concentrated on the boys and girls as they were led to a platform where all could see them.

Loma lifted his eyes to the people, then glanced quickly away. Suddenly he looked again, glancing sideways at the strange-looking man with pale hair on his head and face. Their eyes met and held, for only a second. It was hard for the boy to believe that someone had eyes the color of the sky, hair liked tasseled corn, and skin of white clay. The man must be of the other world, thought Loma. His head was like the painted mask of a kachina spirit.

There was a hammering on the desk. The people stopped talking. "We have fourteen children and a young woman," the leader of the soldiers said to the people. "They are thin from the long journey to Santa Fe. But they are hard workers, bred to work in the fields and to herd sheep." He pushed Butterfly Girl to the front of the group. "We shall start with the prize. What am I bid?"

"Twenty pesos!" yelled a voice from the crowd.

"Thirty!" shouted another.

The bidding went on. Finally Butterfly Girl was sold to a rancher and his family to be used as a servant girl in the big house.

When all of the girls were sold, the young soldier led Loma forward on the platform. In Spanish the soldier said, "This boy is smart. He knows words in Spanish. He can do the work of three youths, you can see how strong he is. I will start the bidding myself with twenty-five pesos."

A murmur went up from the crowd. It was easy to tell that Loma had a strong frame and could endure hardships. The other children kept their eyes to the floor. Loma stared straight ahead, not at the crowd but through and beyond them. His body was there, being bid for with money. But Loma himself would never be a slave. The eyes that looked beyond the milling crowd were the eyes of an independent spirit.

The bidding continued. Finally the young soldier said, "I have been bid ninety pesos. If that is the last bid, this boy goes to . . ."

From the edge of the crowd, a heavy voice boomed, "One hundred pesos!"

"Sold!"

The big man dressed in buckskin pulled out a roll of bills, counted them out to the young soldier, took Loma by the arm and walked him out of the crowded room into the snow-covered street.

14

The big mountain man looked down at the boy's bare feet. He said, "First off, we've got to get you some warm clothes. Come on."

He pulled Loma down the street. They rounded a corner and stopped in front of the Santa Fe Trading Post. The big man opened the door for Loma to enter. The boy planted both feet in the snow refusing to move.

The mountain man frowned. "Look, boy. I don't speak Spanish so good. English is my native tongue. I don't speak any of the Injun languages except a few words I picked up from the plains Injuns while I was crossing the country. So I guess you and me can't communicate much. Leastwise not yet." He pointed through the trading post door to a stack of clothes piled on a back shelf. "See those clothes inside the store? Well, that's what I aim to get for you. Understand?"

Loma refused to budge.

The big man sighed. "Well, all right, if that's the way you want it." He picked Loma up over his shoulder and carried him bodily into the trading post.

The storekeeper uncrossed his legs from the desk top, tipped his chair forward and stood up. A grin crossed his face. "Buenos dias, Senor."

The big man leaned over and sat Loma down on the counter with a thud. "I'm going to need a pair of pants, a shirt, and a pair of moccasins." He nodded at Loma. "His size."

The Spanish storekeeper nodded his head in a rapid series of dips and continued to grin.

"Hmmm. I don't suppose you speak English?" the big man asked.

The grin widened.

"That's what I was afraid of. Okay, I'll look around."

Loma watched the big man go behind the counter, look through the pile of clothes and scratch his reddish-blond beard. When he was certain the man was not looking, he leaped from the counter and started for the door. He was halfway out of the building when he felt a powerful hand on his shoulder.

"Oh no you don't. Listen, boy, I paid good money for you. In return you are going to help me set my beaver traps and learn to tan out the hides. There'll be no running away from me. Got that?" He smiled, a broad smile that lighted up his blue eyes. "You've got spunk. I'll give you that much."

Slowly Loma turned back into the store. He wished he could understand what the big man with corn-tassel hair was saying. His voice was heavier and louder than any he had heard. It reminded him of thunder roaring across the sky.

"Hey!" the mountain main roared. "Lookie here!" He held out a pair of buckskin trousers and a shirt. "That's what I call luck. Never saw buckskin clothes in these parts before. By golly, looks like they'll fit you, too." He took down the buckskin shirt and pants from where they hung on a peg behind a bridle and saddle blanket.

Loma looked away as the big man held them up to him for size. "Good. I think they're going to fit. Take off those rags you're wearing, boy. Here, I'll help you."

With clumsy fingers the trapper fumbled with Loma's tattered clothes. Finally he removed what was left of the cloth shirt and motioned Loma to lift his arms in the air. Then he slipped the buckskin shirt over the arms and pulled it down over the boy's shoulders and chest. "There now. How's that?"

Loma looked at the shirt. He felt it cautiously with his

fingers, touching the soft hide lightly. The trapper with a voice like thunder pointed to Loma's trousers. "Want me to help you with those too?"

The words were meaningless, but the gesture was clear. Quickly Loma slipped the trousers off and held them to the big man. "By golly, you *are* smart. Okay, try these on," he said handing the buckskin pants to the boy.

Loma stepped into the warm leather pants. His own people raised cotton for their clothes. Animal hides were used only for footwear and ceremonial equipment. He lifted his shirt and tied the leather thong tightening the pants around his waist.

"Well, what do you know? A little baggy maybe, but a pretty good fit at that. Now we need some good tough moccasins high enough to cover your ankles. Won't do to have cold feet, and there's plenty of snow where we're going."

Loma's dark eyes opened wide when the trapper handed him a pair of roughside-out moccasins. A long time had passed since his feet were warm. He stroked the moccasins tenderly before slipping them on. Then he stood up and looked down at himself. The heat of the trading post began to close in on him. Quickly he untied the strings on the shirt.

"Oh no you don't. You'll be plenty glad to have those warm clothes once we get outside. One more thing. Set this on that mop of hair for size."

He reached out to fit a beaver fur hat on Loma. The boy shrank back. His people wore no headgear except feathers during the ceremonial dances. He would not wear an animal skin on his head.

"Here now. Take it easy. You and me both got hair enough to cover our ears. But setting traps in a blizzard calls for more than human hair. One time I got the tips of my ears plumb froze off for forgetting to wear my hat. Lookie here.'' He pulled back the reddish-blond hair, bent down a little and showed Loma the missing tip of one ear.

But Loma refused. An animal skin such as that one was to hang from a sash worn only for special ceremonies. It was not to be worn on the head.

The big man let out a deep breath. "Okay, if you won't, you won't. But I'm going to buy it anyhow. Once in the mountains you'll come around to my way of thinking.'' He took Loma by the arm and led him to the counter.

The Spanish storekeeper stood, still grinning.

The trapper gave the storekeeper a quizzical glance. "Well, I guess that'll be all. How much do I owe you?'' He pulled out a roll of pesos and waited.

The storekeeper tallied up the bill and handed it across the counter.

The big man counted out the money, then added two centavos. "Give me a couple of candies,'' he said pointing to the jar.

The storekeeper nodded happily, lifted the lid off the jar and held the jar of candy out to the boy.

Loma looked at the jar, puzzled. He looked up at the big man who nodded for him to take one. Loma didn't know what to do, so he looked away. The trapper stuck his large hand in the jar and took out two candies. He raised Loma's face upward with one hand. "Now watch.'' He put one candy in his mouth. "Here, you do the same.''

Loma took the candy in his hand. For a long while he held it out in front of him, eyeing it. Then he smelled it. Slowly, he turned his back on the two men and put the candy to the tip of his tongue. His eyes brightened. He put the candy in his mouth and turned back around. The look in his dark eyes expressed his pleasure.

"Hmmm," said the big man. "Better give me a bagful." He tossed a handful of centavos on the counter.

The storekeeper nodded rapidly, wrapped the candies in brown paper and handed them to the mountain man.

"Okay, let's get out of here before I've got no money left. Here, this is for you." He pushed the bag of candy into Loma's hand.

Once outside in the snow Loma looked down at his feet. It was the first time in many days they had been warm. The wind blew through the open street. Loma lifted his head. He waited a long time for the wind's magic to come to him as it always had before. But today was not the same. There was no magic in the wind. There was only the howling, the low voice of loneliness.

The big man frowned. "What's the matter with you now? I never in my life saw one for standing still and looking into space so much. Come along. I got a lady friend who's promised us a home-cooked meal before we take off from town to the mountains. Looks to me as you could use it." He pulled Loma along.

The boy clutched the bag of candy tighter. As they walked along he listened to the snow crunch beneath his new moccasins. It reminded him of home when he and his father would race down the steep mesa path on a snowy day, their hair flying in the wind, the fresh taste of snow on their faces and their breath like white smoke against the sky. At the bottom of the mesa they would look at each other, their hearts filled with winter joy. This day was that kind of day, but in a different world. It held no joy.

They walked the length of the street to the edge of town, then took a path that wound among rock boulders into a clearing. They passed three houses. At the fourth house the big man stopped, opened the gate and entered the small yard. Before knocking on the door, the man removed his fur hat, ran his rough hands through his long hair and cleared his throat.

The door opened, framing a young woman with bronze-colored skin, shiny black hair and blue eyes. Loma stared. She had many of the characteristics of his own people, except her skin was shades lighter and her eyes were blue. She smiled and stepped back for them to enter.

"Well, Josie, I got me one. He's a mite young, but he's strong and smart. With me doing the teaching, he'll be a good trapper in no time. This year we'll be working twice as many traps as I could work by myself. With the extra money I'll make, you and I can sure enough get married."

The woman smiled. "What is his name?"

"His name?" asked the big man surprised. "Never thought to ask. I'll pin something on him one of these days."

She touched the big man's shoulder. "As you pinned Josie to me," she said gently.

"Sure. Shucks, I'm not going to call you One Who Carries Corn every time I say your name. Josie is shorter. Besides, Josie is a good name. You like it all right, don't you?"

"If you like it, the name is good. This boy is a Pueblo Indian. But he is not Tewa or Zuni." Her voice was soft.

"Maybe he's Hopi. The Spanish soldiers brought them from the high mesas hundreds of miles from nowhere."

"But why?" she asked, startled. "The Hopi are a peaceful people. It is wrong to capture their children."

The big man shrugged his shoulders. "I suppose it was easier to get Hopi kids than Navajo. The Navajos fight back. Fact is, the Navajos usually end up stealing the Spaniards' horses, leaving the poor devils on foot." He laughed.

She shook her head. "It is wrong. The Hopi people have much power. They love their children. They will want them back."

"Josie, you worry too much. The Hopis live more than five hundred miles from here, perched up on top of high mesas. The only animals they own are sheep and I can't see them riding their sheep all the way to Santa Fe for a bunch of kids."

"The Hopi do not need to ride," she said. "They run many miles without tiring." She turned to the boy and spoke to him in Tewa. "What is your name?"

Loma looked at her. The language was not his, but it was similar. Her eyes told him the words he did not understand.

"Loma," he answered softly.

"My name is One Who Carries Corn. My mother is Tewa. My father was white. It is good to be born into two cultures. It helps one to learn."

Loma partly understood. He nodded. "I am Hopi."

"What is your clan?"

"The Bear Clan."

"And your village?"

"Oraibi."

She smiled. "Are you hungry?"

The boy lowered his eyes to his feet.

"His name is Loma," she explained to the big trapper.

"Loma, huh? What else did you find out?"

"That is all."

"You've been mighty long-winded for just one word," he laughed. "Did you tell him my name?"

"No."

"Why not?"

"It did not occur to me that he did not know." She turned to Loma. "This man," she pointed to him, "his name is Big Jim."

Loma looked from the woman to the man and back to the woman. "Big Jim," he said slowly.

"Good boy!" roared Big Jim. "Now let's eat!"

Loma had never sat on a chair. He had never eaten from a table. Josie placed the steaming hot food on the table, and she and Big Jim sat down. Loma stood watching.

"Come. Sit," she said in Tewa.

Loma looked at the bag of candy still in his hand. He did not move.

She patted the chair with her hand. In Tewa she explained, "This is a chair. As you sit on the rocks in the desert, so we sit on the wooden chairs." She placed her hand on the table. "This is a table. In Oraibi you eat from the floor of your house. In Santa Fe we eat from the table. They are much the same. Come, sit."

Loma looked at the chair, the table, and the woman. Finally he moved forward and silently sat down on the chair. It seemed strange not to cross his legs. He was afraid to move for fear the chair would break or fall over.

Big Jim laughed. "He looks like a scared bird perched on a limb in a wind storm. Relax, boy, and dig in."

Loma watched as the woman and the man lifted food to their mouths on strange-looking sticks. He took a piece of bread in his hand, dipped it in the mutton stew and ate. Big

Jim grinned. "I'll give the Injuns credit. They don't mess around with knives and forks. They eat food like it was supposed to be eaten, with their fingers."

After dinner Loma ate the candy from the brown paper bag while Big Jim and Josie talked and drank coffee. He listened closely, trying to understand their words. Sometimes Jose would translate for him.

Before they left the house, Josie asked, "How long will you be gone this time?"

"'Til spring. I've missed a couple weeks of good trapping already. 'Course it was worth it, I bought me a boy and got to see my woman."

"Where will you go for your trapping?"

"Don't rightly know. We'll follow the big stream into the mountains, then go where the beaver are wintering. I was talking to Beaver Charlie the other day. He said the good trapping is high up on the ridge."

"You will take good care of the boy and keep him warm?"

"Josie, I swear you're worried more about him than about me."

"That is not true." She smiled with her eyes.

"Beaver Charlie offered me his cabin shack. He's spending the winter in Santa Fe. Says he's too old, the cold up there makes his joints stiff. Maybe . . ." he pondered, "maybe I'll just take him up on it. Might even get through the winter without frostbite. Yep, might just do that."

"I would like knowing you are safe and warm," she said.

"Fact is," he went on, "if you see Beaver Charlie, tell him the boy and me are using his cabin. Will you do that for me?"

"Yes."

"By golly, it's getting late. Come on, boy. We've got to hit the trail."

"Do you have supplies?" she asked.

"Yep. They're in the stable with the horses. Probably take me half the night to teach Loma . . . is that his name? Yeah, Loma . . . to pack the horses."

"You will not wait for morning?"

"Can't. Horses' board is paid up through today. Had to buy another packhorse. Haven't got but a little money left, and that's for you."

Josie knew better than to argue. Big Jim always left her a certain amount of money and he wouldn't take "no" for an answer. It meant much for him to have someone who cared, somebody he could depend on. He asked nothing in return. It was a point of honor with him. Before next year they would be married. He had agreed to the marriage ceremony of her people. Josie was grateful.

"My thoughts will be with you," she said.

He rose from the chair and kissed her. Then, without a word, he grabbed his fur hat, took Loma by the arm, and walked out of the house into the night.

It was a long, cold trip into the mountains. Big Jim made Loma wear a heavy bearskin covering to keep warm. The boy was not pleased. His entire body was wrapped in the skins of dead animals. The smell of death still lingered in the bearskin. In his mind he could see the innocent bear eating from a berry bush. He saw him jump and leap and bound to get away from the man who held death in a shooting stick. The sound of the explosion echoed in his ears, the same sound he had heard that terrible morning in his village. And then the bear lay dead, his breath taken away by the wind as his spirit climbed the ladder out of the top of his head to free itself from the empty shell of no life.

The nose cannot smell without the mind, thought Loma. I will send my thoughts away. And he tried to make his mind go beyond the earth, beyond the clouds, beyond the sky, to the force behind the sun. But he could not. He was bound to the smell of the bearskin.

"By golly," roared Big Jim. "We're making better time than I thought. Best give the horses a rest. They're blowing pretty hard."

He dismounted and motioned Loma to do the same. The boy slipped quietly from the horse and pressed his hand gently against the horse's sweaty neck. The horse was real, it had the smell of life. The wet hair was warm beneath his touch. He stood there not wanting to leave the hard-breathing animal.

"Over here, boy. Help me kick some of the snow off this log so we can sit and eat."

Loma obeyed. He tied the horse to a limb, then moved over to Big Jim and brushed snow from the log.

"Now, boy, I don't hanker to spend the rest of the winter talking to myself, so I aim to teach you some words in English. First off, this here is bread. Bread, got it?" He held the loaf in front of Loma. "Bread."

Loma understood. He nodded.

"No. Say it. Say bread." He put his big hand to Loma's lips. "Bread."

"Bread," said Loma simply.

"Humph. Why didn't you say so before if it's that easy? Trying to make a donkey out of me? Okay, this here is jerky. Dried beef. Say it."

"Jerkydriedbeef."

"No." He held up three fingers. "It's three words. Jerky . . . dried . . . beef."

"Jerky. Dried. Beef." Loma said so softly that Big Jim could hardly hear him.

"Yeah, I think that's okay. Talk up. How do you expect me to teach you if you mumble everything I say?" He pointed to a pine tree. "Know what that is?"

"Arbol," Loma replied.

"Naw. That's Spanish. In English it's *tree.*"

"Tree?"

"That's right. Pretty good. If your body is as strong as your mind, you'll be setting traps in no time."

While they ate, Big Jim pointed to the snow, the clouds, the sky, the horses, the packs on the horses' backs, the saddles, and their own clothing. As a part of his duty Loma repeated each word.

"Not bad. 'Course if you're like me, you'll forget them by tomorrow and we'll have to start all over. Let's tighten the cinches and be on our way."

Big Jim showed Loma how to smooth the blanket under the saddle and tighten the cinch. They mounted, untied the pack horses and continued up the mountain, breaking a trail as they went. As they rode beneath the tall pines, Loma whispered each word he had learned over and over. He would not forget.

The higher they went, the deeper the snow. In places it was up to the horses' knees. They camped in a small clearing. Big Jim and Loma cleared away the snow and Big Jim built a fire.

Loma sat down, wound his arms around his knees and tried to picture what his mother and father were doing now. In his memory he could hear the wind sweeping across the mesa, leaving it clean and fresh. His father would be in the kiva with the men of his clan teaching the laws of Creation and telling stories. The boys his own age would be in the kiva with the men, listening to the stories and learning about the road of life. This was the year he would have been initiated into the Powamu Society. Last year he had made the pilgrimage to the Salt Cave in the Grand Canyon. Initiation into Powamu Society was the most important initiation in their religious lives. He would miss it. His father would be sad, for he was the kiva chief and had looked forward to Loma's initiation since the day the boy was born. And Loma was sad, for Powamu was the purification ceremony for all life.

Big Jim took a buffalo robe from one of the pack horses, sat down near Loma and wrapped the heavy robe around them.

"We'll be needing this before morning," he said. "Now, let's get on with some new words. This here is a buffalo robe. Say it."

"Buflow."

"Buff-a-lo," Big Jim corrected, separating the syllables.

"Buff-a-lo."

"Good. Say it again."

"Buff-a-lo."

"Well, doggone if I shouldn't've been a school teacher."

For nearly an hour they went over words. Finally Big Jim stretched his large frame out on part of the buffalo robe. "That's enough for tonight, I'm wore out. Lie down now and go to sleep. Don't get any ideas about running off, 'cause I sleep with one ear and one eye open."

By the tone of Jim's voice, Loma knew that the trapper meant him to lie down and not try to get away.

The next morning the sun came. Loma lifted his eyes to welcome it. They fed the horses, saddled two, and tied the packs on the other three. Big Jim and Loma ate breakfast on the trail as the horses plunged through the deep snow up the mountain.

All day there was no wind, no movement in the trees, no sound except for the heavy breathing of the horses as they broke trail through the soft snow. Loma listened to the music of the silence. He could almost feel the mountain breathing beneath his horse's hoofs. Big Jim was somewhat like the mountain, big and wild and free. The boy liked him and he didn't like him. Big Jim was a mystery to him.

Later in the afternoon when the shadows stole across the glistening snow, Big Jim removed his fur hat and slapped it happily against his leg. "The stream!" he bellowed. The horse under him jumped nervously. "What am I doing a trapper? I should have been a trailblazer. I sure should've!"

Loma's horse tugged at the bit, anxious to drink from the rushing water. The boy gave the horse his head.

"Up yonder, not more than four or five days from here, is the cabin shack. Meanwhile, if we see any likely looking prospects, we'll set out the traps. With the heavy winter we're having, the beaver pelts will be the best ever."

Loma pointed to the rapid-flowing water. "What name?" he asked.

"Stream, boy. Stream. Not big enough to be a river and too big for a creek. It's called a stream, boy, and it's loaded with beaver!"

Loma looked at Big Jim, his dark eyes unblinking. Had the man of mystery never seen water before to show such pleasure? Then he turned to the stream and watched his horse drink. He watched each swallow travel down the horse's throat and disappear just as he had seen shadows disappear when the sun slipped behind the mountain peaks.

During the night, heavy clouds drifted in and settled on the mountains. By morning it was snowing. Big Jim looked out from under the buffalo robe. Suddenly he jumped up.

"Hurry, boy. There's a blizzard coming. We've got to head for the cabin. Can't be wasting time setting traps on the way. Hurry up."

Together they saddled and packed the horses. Before snow covered the ground where they had lain, they were on their horses riding north toward the cabin.

The day was cold and gray; wind blew snow flurries up from the ground, down from the sky. They followed the stream northward through the fat spruce timberland. They paused for rest at the top of a steep bank. Loma looked back along the trail they had come; it was covered over with white. Even the ice along the side of the stream was built up with snow. The stream curved and twisted away into the north, disappearing behind islands of huge rock when only the rushing waters could be heard.

It was more snow than Loma had ever seen. There was no longer music in its silence. The cold crept in. The horses plunged in among the big spruce trees. A foot of snow fell between morning and night. When darkness covered the mountain, Big Jim called over his shoulder to the boy riding hunched against the falling snow.

"There won't be any stopping for us tonight. Too cold. We'll be lucky to beat out this blizzard as it is. Can you understand? We won't be stopping."

Loma's eyes questioned him.

"Dad gum it, now listen. No sleep tonight. We'll follow the stream. Got to keep going or we'll get frostbite." He made motions with his hands.

"Ride all night," Loma said.

"What? Speak up."

Loma nodded to show he understood. Then he bent his

head down and patted the horse's warm neck. In Hopi he said, "It is sad to make you walk so far. I am sorry."

When they stopped at last, the next afternoon, Big Jim told Loma to care for the horses while he climbed up a steep bank. On top, tangled in the underbrush near the trunk of a large spruce tree was a wind deposit of half dry firewood. He gathered sticks and twigs. Some of the larger pieces he threw down the bank on the snow. The rest he bundled in his arms and slid down the steep bank to the bottom. He dug a hole in the snow and arranged the twigs for the fire. He fed the flame until it was going well, then carefully laid one of the larger sticks across the blazing twigs.

Loma joined him and they ate dinner squatting beside the fire in the snow. "Get some sleep," Big Jim insisted. "I'll keep the fire going. We'll trade off."

The tired boy slept without thinking, without dreaming. The only move he made was to curl tighter into a ball. He awoke to Big Jim's hand upon his shoulder. "Keep the fire going. I need to get a couple hours shut-eye before we take off again."

Loma wrapped the bearskin tightly around him. For the first time he was thankful for having it. By now he was used to the smell.

Toward dawn Loma could no longer feed the fire. The wood was gone. Before the fire died out completely he crept away from camp to look for firewood. As he made his way through the darkness the wind lulled. Drifts of snow, shaken from the long pine boughs, glided like wings of birds and settled on him as he walked beneath the trees. There was no light, the moon was hidden behind night clouds. Loma groped his way along in the dark.

Big Jim turned over in the heavy buffalo robe and opened one sleep-filled eye toward the dying fire. In an instant he was on his feet. The boy was gone! He threw the buffalo robe to the ground and started headlong through the snow. Anger gripped him, giving new strength to his legs as he plunged forward. "Shouldn't've trusted him," he mumbled. "Sneaky little Injun. First time I close my eyes on him, he runs away. Won't make it far in this blizzard, he'll freeze to death. Serve him right."

Big Jim stopped to listen. In the distance he heard the cracking of twigs. He ran forward, leaping and bounding through the snow. Then he saw him. The big man lunged forward, caught Loma around the legs and pulled him to the ground. "Thought you could run away from Big Jim, huh?" he growled, breathing heavily.

Loma turned his face away from the snow and looked up at him. "No life in fire. I get wood," he said simply.

The realization of the boy's words, half in Hopi, half in English caused Big Jim to release the legs. He stood up, brushed the snow from his clothes. "You'd better be right. Where's the wood?"

Slowly Loma pushed up from the deep snow. Before brushing himself off, he pointed to a small pile of twigs and sticks only a few feet from them. He watched Big Jim pick the pile of sticks up in his arms and head back to camp. Loma followed.

In another hour they saddled up and moved north again, following the stream through the mountain. Two hours later when the first light of day should have brightened the horizon, the sky was hidden by a subtle gloom that made the day dark. By midmorning a dry, cold wind blew low across the mountains, whirling the fresh snow upward, blinding their eyes to what lay before them.

32

"Give your horse his head," yelled Big Jim through the swirling snow. "Won't do to try to guide him through this." He turned in the saddle and saw Loma's head covered with snow. Reining in his horse, he pulled the fur cap out of the saddlebag and waited for Loma to ride up beside him.

The boy looked out of the corners of his eyes, not wanting to raise his head to the blasting wind. Big Jim reached out with the fur hat. "Here, put this on. Cover your nose by burying it in the bearskin. Do as I say. If you leave your nose and ears uncovered, you'll end up without any. Understand?"

Loma understood that he was to wear the fur hat. As much as he was opposed to it, he accepted the hat and pulled it on. His ears had been cold a while ago, but now they had no feeling and he didn't know if they were cold or not. After wearing the fur hat for a short time, his ears began to tingle and ache. He knew then that they had been numb and were thawing out. Big Jim was wise to make him wear the hat.

Loma felt the legs of his tired horse weaken under him. The boy's heart went out to the animal. The deep snow and the upward climb had sapped the horse's strength. Loma dismounted, took the reins in his hand and walked beside the horse. Time after time the boy sank into snowdrifts above his knees almost to his waist. He leaned forward to scramble out of the soft snow. In only a few minutes his breath was coming in short gasps. But for the first time in days he felt the blood running quickly through his body, feeding him with a comfortable warmth.

"What in the name of all that's holy are you doing?" Big Jim roared. "Get back on that horse!"

Loma raised his eyes to the man. In the depth of the dark eyes Big Jim saw the boy's determination. Loma said nothing, but he did not get on the horse.

"You stubborn little . . ." But the man didn't finish. His own horse buckled at the knees and went down on the snow. Big Jim jumped off before he was pinned under the saddle. The horse struggled up to his feet and stood trembling. "All right. You win. I don't aim to kill me no horses unless I have to."

He handed the reins of his horse to Loma, then waded through the snow to one of the packhorses where he removed two pairs of snowshoes from the pack. He handed a pair of the flat leather-thonged shoes to Loma. "Ever worn snowshoes before?" he asked.

"Snowshoes?" Loma tried the strange word on his tongue.

"Yeah. They're made so that a man can walk atop the snow instead of sinking through the stuff. Watch how I put them on."

He leaned against his horse to fasten first one snowshoe and then the other. He shuffled forward a few steps to show Loma how they worked. "Okay, got it?"

"Snowshoes," Loma repeated, amazed.

"Yeah. Now put them on. Here, I'll help."

Big Jim took the shoes from the boy, knelt down and fastened them to the moccasined feet. Loma tried to take a step, but the long heel of the shoe caught in the snow and he couldn't move.

"That ain't the way to do it. Weren't you watching me? Now look careful, 'cause we're wasting precious time."

Big Jim bent his knees and, barely lifting his feet from the snow, shuffled along. "Try again," he said.

Loma took a deep breath, bent his knees and moved one large snowshoe in front of the other. He looked up.

"You'll get used to it. Take your horse and let's make tracks. I don't like the looks of this sky."

As the dark day merged into night, the temperature dropped. Big Jim strapped a piece of fur across the boy's nose and across his own. On and on they went. Loma thought his legs would not take another step. The fur kept his nose from getting frostbitten, but his cheeks felt numb. He could not go on. Without a word he sank to the snow and closed his eyes to rest. Suddenly he felt a heavy mittened hand slap his face. His eyes flew open. Big Jim was standing in front of him removing the snowshoes.

"Get on that horse!" he demanded. "And stay there. You hear?"

Loma staggered to his feet and shook his head. "I walk," he said in a hoarse voice.

"Don't give me more trouble than I already got." He lifted the boy to the horse. "Now stay there! It's not so many more hours before we reach the cabin."

Big Jim tied the reins of the boy's horse in a knot over the snow-covered mane. "Leave the reins be. He'll follow."

A strange feeling came over Loma. He didn't know if he could stay on the plunging horse. As he sat there swaying in the saddle, a vision came to him. He saw his mother and father deep in meditation sending strength to their son. The vision seemed bathed in pure light, and from the bottom of his mind he sensed a snake winding itself upward through his body and out the top of his head; and when it touched the light of the vision the snake became a winged antelope that raised itself upward taking him with it. Then he was on the antelope's back soaring through space, joining the force of his mother and father. He was with them and he was not with them, but he was no longer so exhausted. The vision disappeared as quickly as it came. He raised his bouncing head and sat straighter in the saddle.

It was cold. The boy batted his arms across his chest and against his legs. Moving his fingers seemed impossible, so he concentrated on bending each one back and forth over and over again. He did the same with his toes. How many hours they had traveled since night fell, the boy did not know. He felt the bitter wind sting against his face and he listened to the trees moaning in the night. He was vaguely aware of the stream to their left. The snow continued to fall, whirling in the wind from the sky downward and from the earth upward. Suddenly his horse stopped.

"We made it!" called Big Jim. "Do you hear me, boy? We made it!"

Loma peered through the black storm. A faint outline of a cabin stood before them.

"Get down. Let's get inside and build us a fire."

Loma slid from the horse. But he made no attempt to walk into the cabin.

"You deaf? I said let's go inside."

Loma shook his head. "The horses," he insisted.

"We'll tend to them in the morning. Come on."

The boy refused. He removed the fur mittens and worked at the stiff leather latigo strap to uncinch the saddle. He would not leave the horses standing in the blizzard.

"What's the matter, your brain freeze up?"

The words poured forth in Hopi. "The horses have given their hearts to bring us here. They are hungry and tired. We must care for them." He fumbled with the latigo strap.

"That's a mighty bunch of words coming from such a closed-mouthed kid. Too bad I don't know what you're talking about."

"Horses," repeated Loma. "Hungry."

"Boy, if you don't beat all. Here we are standing out in a blizzard freezing to death when the makings of a good fire are only a couple feet away and you want to take care of a bunch of critters. Well, go ahead if you insist; there's a shed over yonder." He pointed. "I'm going in to thaw out."

Loma led the horses in the direction Big Jim had pointed. Soon he was near a shed. Though it was too dark to see, he found the door and groped his way inside. After a long struggle he finally had the horses unsaddled and unpacked. One of the horses nickered low and walked over to a storage room piled high with hay. Loma climbed through a small opening and threw out enough hay for the five horses. It was cold in the shed, but the snow and wind were outside. The horses would be comfortable if they stood close together and shared their body warmth. Loma patted each one on the neck, then walked out into the blizzard toward the cabin.

For two days the blizzard raged, piling snow in high banks against the cabin. Loma spent the first day with the horses in the shed. He made a makeshift brush out of straw and curried the horses until their long winter coats shone. He separated the knotted strands in their manes and tails and talked to them in Hopi about his home on the high mesas in the painted desert.

"In the winter," he told them, "when it is cold and the plants do not grow, it is time for Mother Earth to rest. It is then that our people are kept busy with sacred ceremonies that tell the story of Creation. There is much prayer and meditation. Our hearts must be pure or bad forces may enter our villages and land."

He stopped brushing the horse in front of him and climbed up onto the feedbox. "Would you like to know the things that our people do? Good, then I will tell you. The men go to the kivas to tell stories. And they weave blankets, carve kachina dolls and make masks for the ceremonies. It is in the kiva that the older men give instructions to children. Their words have much power and wisdom and we must listen closely and learn to keep our hearts pure. In the winter, the women of Oraibi make beautiful baskets and grind corn for piki bread and for use in the ceremonies.''

The horses responded to his soft voice by moving closer to him. Loma smiled. Talking to the horses about his home filled him with happiness. In a dreamy voice he continued. ''We call the kivas the world below because they are built below the ground deep in the body of Mother Earth. At night we make a fire in the kiva to keep warm. It is then I watch the smoke rise out of Mother Earth into the heavens to meet the stars. And . . .''

''Hey, boy!'' Big Jim stuck his bearded face in the shed. ''I brought you up here to help me, not to sit around gabbing with the horses all day. We've got to take these packs into the cabin and unload supplies. Give me a hand.''

Loma laid the straw brush aside, hopped down from the feedbox and went to the man. They carried the packs from the shed to the cabin where they unloaded the food supplies and trapping equipment. Big Jim set the traps out on the floor. They were made out of heavy metal weighing over five pounds apiece. Loma frowned when he saw them.

''What are you scowling about?'' Big Jim boomed in the thunderous voice. ''These here traps are going to make me plenty of money. Fact is, they're going to make me rich!''

Loma stared at him.

As Big Jim laid the traps out on the cabin floor his excitement grew. ''Don't you see, boy? With this hard winter we're having the beaver pelts will be good and thick. Five dollars a pound they're bringing. Five dollars! No reason to waste time; starting tomorrow I'll teach you to pack the possible sack. Doesn't look like the blizzard's going to let up before then. The following day, providing the weather turns, we'll start setting the traps along the stream.''

Loma's eyes grew round. He had seen Big Jim happy twice, once with Josie and now with the traps. He liked the happiness at Josie's house. He did not like the happiness with the traps.

"First of all we'll pack the possible sack!"

"Possible sack?"

"Yep. That's this here bag. It carries everything possible a trapper might need. But that's for tomorrow. Right now I've got a hollow in my belly a foot deep. When the weather clears I'll shoot a deer. Till then we'll have to make out with beans.''

The next morning Loma woke early. He started a fire in the fireplace, then left the cabin to feed the horses. When he returned, Big Jim was up, boiling a pot of coffee.

"Sky is still dark as the underside of a turtle, but the storm's let up some,'' Big Jim said, pouring out two cups of coffee. "If the wind dies down by tonight I'll be on my way to making real money.''

Loma sat down to the coffee and plate of cold beans. He ate slowly, without enthusiasm. Although he had never seen how a beaver trap worked, the thought of the iron teeth biting into an animal saddened him. And Big Jim had made no prayer sticks. How, he thought, can an animal be asked for his life without a prayer stick?

Big Jim didn't notice the boy's sadness. When he finished eating he said, "Come over here and I'll give you the first lesson in packing a possible sack.''

Loma rose quietly from the chair. He knew that the word 'come' meant Big Jim wanted him. He knelt beside the mountain man and watched.

"First off a man packs an extra pair of moccasins."

Loma's eyes questioned him.

"Sure. Beaver won't come if they smell human, so we got to wade up the stream to get rid of the man smell before setting the traps. Understand?"

Loma didn't.

"Humph. Well, I'm telling you that an extra pair of dry moccasins are needed and I know what I'm about. Of course we got to take flint along for fire."

Loma nodded.

"Well, I'm glad you understand something. The buffalo robe goes in and some chewing tobacco for me; these wooden pegs for the traps, then last of all the traps themselves." He stood back. "Oh, yeah. Can't forget the hatchet." He tucked it in the bag.

Loma said nothing.

"The rest of the stuff I carry on my person. In my belt go a couple of knives used for skinning beaver and," he laughed, "for scalping Injuns. But don't worry, I ain't planning to scalp any redskins around here. Most of 'em are pretty peaceful. In the plains country it was a different story. Never did fancy scalping a man much. But there's no use leaving their hair when you're paid for bringing it in."

Loma looked away.

"This here pistol goes in my belt, too. Never know when a man's going to need a pistol. The powder horn and bullet pouch go over my shoulder. Ever shoot a gun, boy? Nope, don't suppose you ever have. Well, they're mighty handy."

"Now there's one important thing I haven't told you about yet. This here is castoreum. Say it."

"Castorum."

"No. You forgot the 'e'. Cas-tor-e-um."

Loma formed the word on his lips and whispered, "Cas-tor-e-um."

Big Jim strained to hear him. "Practice that word, you'll be using it a lot. I'll admit this here castoreum doesn't look like much more than a yellowish oil. But it's potent. We get it from the glands of beavers. We bait the trap by setting an aspen twig just above the water and smearing it with castoreum. The beaver can't help but be attracted by the scent, so he swims up to the bait and WHAM! The trap springs shut." He clapped his hands together for emphasis.

The words were deadly and cold. Loma rose to look out the window and calm the war in his heart.

Big Jim unpacked the possible sack and called Loma over to repack it. He had the boy name each article as he put it in. Three times he unpacked it, and three times Loma named the contents as he repacked the sack. Big Jim was pleased with the quickness of Loma's mind, but he didn't like the way he handled the traps.

"They ain't going to bite you, boy. Take hold of 'em like you mean business."

That afternoon Loma went into the shed with the horses. For a long time he sat on the edge of the feedbox thinking. He wanted to send good thoughts out to the beavers explaining why Big Jim must kill them, but he couldn't.

"My people," he told the horses, "kill animals because they need food for their stomachs and skins for the ceremonies. Our prayers ask the animal spirits to understand what they must do and to have no fear. The hearts and thoughts of the hunter must be pure before the animals can willingly give their earthly lives to help the people. Big Jim has made no prayer sticks. I do not think his heart is pure.''

After feeding the horses, Loma removed the buckskin shirt and pants. He took off the moccasins and unwrapped the blanket cloth around the bottom parts of his legs and feet. When he was entirely naked, he walked out of the shed into the snow.

Big Jim stood at the cabin window checking the weather. The wind had calmed and only soft snow flurries fluttered down from the sky. He grinned, satisfied that tomorrow he could set the traps. Suddenly he noticed a movement in the snow near the shed. Eyes squinted in disbelief, he stared out of the window. There was Loma washing himself in the snow.

"He's crazy!" Big Jim mumbled to himself. "I bought me a crazy Injun." He walked to the cabin door and stuck his head out to get a better view. "Taking a bath in the snow. If that doesn't beat all. Sure enough the boy's gone loco!"

When Loma returned fully dressed to the cabin, Big Jim rubbed his large hand through his reddish-blond beard. "Boy," he said slowly, "were my eyes deceiving me or did I see you taking a bath in the snow?"

Loma stared, not understanding.

"It's where you wash yourself all over. Like this." Big Jim went through the motions.

"Oh," Loma said.

"Well. Were you taking a bath or not?"

"Yes."

"What in tarnation for? Do you want to freeze yourself to death?"

"I do not frost."

"You do not frost," grumbled Big Jim. "You mean freeze."

Loma nodded.

Suddenly Big Jim realized that Loma had not smelled bad since they arrived. It was more than he could say for himself. Trying to be inconspicuous he sniffed his own clothes. The odor was awful.

"How often you do that crazy bathing? Today your first time?"

Loma shook his head. "All day."

"You mean *every* day. When are you going to learn to talk right?" He was irritated to think that a young boy bathed when he didn't have to. He was more irritated because he needed a bath and didn't want to take one. He started for the door. "You throw something together for dinner. I'm going to check the weather."

Big Jim was gone longer than was necessary to check weather conditions. Loma poured water from a bucket into an iron kettle, then sprinkled in cornmeal. While he was stirring it over the fire, Big Jim entered. His face was shiny clean, his hair and beard still wet from the snow. "Stopped snowing," he said embarrassed at the knowing glance Loma gave him. "Clouds seem to be lifting a little. Tomorrow we'll get down to business."

Before sunrise Loma was out of the cabin in the shed. He watched intently as the sun came. His hands rose to meet the sun and he experienced the joy of welcoming the great light that warmed the world. Far below the shed he could hear the stream splashing over the rocks as it cut its way through the heart of the high mountains. Gray clouds hung in wisps over the giant spruce trees, and as the sun rose higher it seemed to take the clouds with it farther into the sky. The snow glistened white under the shining light.

Then a shadow covered Loma's heart as he remembered this was the day Big Jim would set the beaver traps. He felt the urge to run away, to hide from the mountain man. But where would he go? He did not know the mountain trails well enough to get out alive. Would some of his people come to Santa Fe to ask for him? If they did, who would know where he was, high up in the mountains? Loma did not have the answers. Slowly, very slowly, he moved back to the cabin. One day the fog would lift. Until then he would wait. Learn and wait.

"Hurry up, boy," Big Jim called from the cabin door. "Time's a-wasting."

Before going inside Loma looked again at the sun and noticed that the black bangs of his square-cut hair hung down to his eyes. He brushed them back, drank the sunlight into his body and went inside.

"Big Jim?"

"Yeah?"

Loma pointed to his long bangs. Then he pointed to the knife in Big Jim's belt.

"No, boy," Big Jim laughed. "No need to worry. I ain't going to scalp you." His thunderous voice roared good-naturedly. "Unless of course you don't behave."

Loma frowned. "No," he said. "Hair long. I wish knife to . . ." He groped for the correct word, "to . . . cut."

Big Jim took the knife from his belt and threw it point down sticking in the cabin floor not more than an inch from Loma's moccasin.

The boy's dark face turned suddenly pale. "Thank you," he said softly. He bent down and worked the sharp knife out of the wood.

Big Jim roared with laughter.

Loma took a shiny tin plate from the cupboard, propped it against the cabin wall and sat down cross-legged in front of it. In a few minutes the long bangs were cut straight and evenly across his forehead.

"Humph," Big Jim grumbled, noticing the skilled job of haircutting. "The way you keep so neat and clean you'd think you were a girl." He pointed to his own long hair and beard. "So long as you're so cutting-happy, make yourself useful and trim this mop of hair. Hurry now, 'cause we've got to be on our way."

Loma nodded, took a handful of the long reddish-blond hair that hung to the man's shoulders and began to cut. "Ouch, dad gum it. Stop pulling."

When Loma had finished with the hair, Big Jim pointed to his beard. "Take some of this off. You know, one time I was out trapping and the weather turned so cold that every time I spit tobacco, the spit froze in midair. Mostly, though, it gets in my beard and freezes there. Don't cut so much as to expose my chin. Don't want to get frostbite."

Loma waited for Big Jim to finish talking.

"Well, boy. What's holding you up?"

"You talk. Face moves."

Big Jim gave him a piercing look. "Cut!" he demanded.

Loma obeyed. When he was through, Big Jim took the tin plate and looked at himself. The beard looked fine, neat and trim. He moved the plate to the side and squinted to get a good look at his hair.

"Banging beavertails!" he shouted. "What are you trying to do, make a Hopi Injun out of me? You've cut my hair smack-dab straight across. What do you think I am?"

Loma stepped back, disappointed. The haircut was good. The men in his village would not complain.

"Give me that knife!"

Loma obeyed. His eyes widened as the mountain man deliberately cut uneven hunks out of the straight, square cut the boy had given him.

"Don't know what the devil I was thinking letting you get ahold of my hair in the first place. Eat your breakfast and meet me outside. Everything's ready." He jammed the beaver hat on his head and stomped out of the cabin.

Wearing snowshoes, the man and boy shuffled over the high snow to the big stream. They walked along in silence, each feeling the day in a different way. Loma breathed in the cold air deeply and with satisfaction. He turned his eyes to the bright winter sun, too far away to give much warmth, but close enough to brighten the world. It was a good day.

As they moved farther upstream, Big Jim pointed to a large dam made of sticks and mud across the stream. "There they are," he said happily.

Loma strained to see the beaver. He saw nothing. "Where?" he questioned.

"Right there ahead. Don't you see their dam?" the big man grumbled.

"I no see . . . beaver," Loma said in broken English.

"Well of course not. They got their homes in the stream banks and stay holed up all day. But they'll be out tonight, by golly, and tomorrow we'll have us some beaver pelts."

Loma stopped at the dam and studied it. Never before had he seen a beaver dam, and he wondered what kind of animal could build with sticks and mud the same as did humans. Big Jim went on ahead and signaled Loma to follow.

The mountain man squatted down. He grinned. "This here is called a steambed."

"Steambed?"

"Yeah. The beaver builds his house here in the bank with tunnels running out below the water. This whole area is called a steambed. That's where we'll set some snares. Now you watch and listen to me while I set these here traps, so you'll know just what to do when your time comes."

Big Jim went downstream, waded into the water, then walked upstream to the steambed where Loma waited. He took out the metal trap and anchored it to a stout wooden stake which he drove into the bank.

Loma looked at him puzzled. In Hopi he asked, "Why are you in water?"

Big Jim looked up from what he was doing. "Huh?"

"You stand in water."

"What do you want me to do, sit down?" he grumbled.

"Why you in water?"

"I told you before, we got to get rid of the human smell or the beaver won't come out to the traps this evening. I thought you were smart enough to remember that."

Big Jim went back to work. He baited the trap by setting an aspen twig just above water level and smearing it with castoreum. "Remember what this stuff is?"

"Castoreum."

Big Jim nodded. "Now when the beaver smells this stuff, he'll swim up to the bait and the trap will spring directly underneath. Got it?"

"How it catch him?"

"By the foot. The beaver will panic and dive into the deep water. The trap will pull him up short. He'll struggle to beat all heck for a while, but it won't do any good. He'll soon drown."

Loma turned away.

Big Jim's forehead wrinkled into a frown. "Any questions?"

Loma shook his head.

"After setting the trap, you got to wade back down the stream." He climbed out of the water, took a dry pair of moccasins out of the possible sack, put them on and motioned to the boy.

Loma came to him. "Help me with the other traps. We'll go upstream a few miles, set what traps we can, then we'll head back down the other side and set the rest of them."

Loma was quiet as they walked along. Finally he asked, "How big beaver?"

"Depends on how old they are. Beavers never stop growing. Did you know that? Some of them live to be ten years old and still they're growing. 'Course they grow pretty slow."

"How big?" Loma repeated softly.

"They get as long as three feet and weigh anywhere from fifty to seventy pounds."

Loma cocked his dark head to one side. He did not understand about feet and pounds.

Big Jim noticed his confusion. He set the possible sack on the ground and stretched out his arms. "About this long," he explained, "and they get about as heavy as a big dog."

The boy's eyes grew round. He must see a beaver. He had thought they were the size of Big Jim's beaverskin hat.

At the next stop, Loma lowered his hand into the stream

water. It was icy cold. He couldn't figure out how a beaver or any animal could live in such cold water without freezing. In his land, the animals came down out of the mountains in the winter to the foothills where the grass was not covered with snow.

"What's bothering you now?" Big Jim boomed.

"Water cold."

"Well sure it's cold. What'd you expect? Doesn't bother the beaver any, if that's what you're thinking. They wear long underwear."

The boy gazed at him intently.

"Sure they do. Oil comes out of their bodies and waterproofs the underwear."

Wonder filled Loma's dark eyes.

"All right, then call it underfur if you want to. All the same, he's got it. And he's got a tail like nothing you've ever seen. When he's cutting down trees, he uses the tail as a prop to keep him upright. When he's making a dam, he uses his tail to smack the mud in place; and when he's swimming, the tail guides him wherever he wants to go. But the best thing about beaver tail is the eating. Roast it in coals until it's ready to pop. Nothing like it, by golly."

Loma tried to keep up with the big man's chatter. Too many words confused him. They walked along the stream to a waterfall. The white spray shot upward like misty smoke, partly hiding the clear stream water. Loma watched a tree limb slide over the falls into the misty spray below. Later it was tossed again to the surface and tumbled down the fast-rushing stream.

All day they walked. When Big Jim could not find a steambed, he chose a site where his own experience or the abundance of beaver signs told him that there were good hunting prospects. It was dark when they arrived again at the cabin. Big Jim removed the snowshoes and went directly inside. Loma turned away from the cabin to the shed. He would not feed himself until he had taken care of the horses.

That night the boy was too tired to take a bath in the snow. After dinner he wrapped up in the buffalo robe and was soon asleep.

At sunrise Loma awoke troubled. Big Jim was up, standing over the small fire stirring a pot of beans and waiting for the coffee to boil. He seemed happy. The sun would shine again today. Suddenly Loma realized that this was the day they would check the traps for beaver. As much as he wanted to see a beaver, he dreaded to see one dead. In his heart he felt it was wrong to kill the way Big Jim killed. The man had said it was for money. Loma did not understand.

Before eating, the boy fed the horses and went over their coats with the homemade straw brush. The horses liked him. Each time he entered the shed, they whinnied and nuzzled him with their soft noses. Talking to the horses pleased Loma more than talking to Big Jim, because the horses understood him even if he did not say a word. They were calm and peaceful; in them was no violence, no desire to kill.

After breakfast, the man and boy strapped on the snowshoes and set out for the stream. Big Jim was tense, anxious to know how many beaver had been trapped. He walked fast, almost at a trot. Loma had a difficult time keeping up with him.

In less than an hour the beaver dam loomed into view. Loma slowed down, afraid of what he might see. But Big Jim hurried all the more. Soon Loma heard the man shout excitedly. Slowly Loma moved forward. Big Jim pulled a big beaver out of the water, took him out of the trap and held him up by the tail, dead.

"Look at that pelt!" he roared. "He must weigh sixty pounds. Just look at that pelt!"

Loma looked, but not at the pelt. His eyes fastened on the hind leg, chewed and torn from the struggle with the trap. The beaver had died in fear and pain.

"Come here, boy. Watch closely while I skin him. If you get good enough, I might let you skin a couple before spring."

Loma squatted down on his haunches, eyes hooded, concentrating on the shadow his head cast on the white snow, while the trapper skillfully skinned the beaver. Loma stared unbelieving when Big Jim threw away, every bit of meat and intestine, saving only the pelt and the tail. Loma's people had always used every part of the animal so there was no waste. The skeleton and hide were used in ceremonies and the meat was eaten. He said nothing, but the troubled feeling that had been with him earlier returned. He looked up to see a swiftly moving cloud cover the sun, turning the bright world gray.

After skinning the beaver, Big Jim walked downstream again and waded up where he reset the trap some distance away. Then he and the boy set off to the next trap. By late afternoon Big Jim had skinned out five beaver. He swore angrily at one trap. The trap pole had not held, and the beaver had been able to drag the trap up onto the bank where he freed himself by gnawing through his snared paw. The remaining part of his leg was still in the trap.

"I'll get you yet, you . . ." Big Jim grumbled as he reset the trap.

Loma was glad the beaver had got away, but he couldn't help wondering if he could live with one of his legs missing.

After setting the trap, Big Jim scowled at Loma. "What's the matter with you anyhow?"

Loma turned away.

Big Jim was angry for having lost the beaver and angrier still at the boy who had been no help at all. "You listen to me when I talk to you!" He grabbed Loma by the shoulder and swung him around.

Loma looked directly into the furious eyes.

"You see this trap chain? Well, I ain't above taking it to you, understand? Grab up those pelts and carry them across the stream."

Loma strained against the weight of the possible sack. The pelts, still heavy with water and fleshy tissue that would not dry for many days, weighed the boy to the point of exhaustion. Three-fourths of the way across the wide, fast-flowing stream, he slipped on a moss-covered rock and fell. He tried to hold the pelt sack, but the swift water took it from his hands to the bottom of the stream. Numbness crept into his limbs as he frantically searched the bottom of the icy stream.

Suddenly there was a rough hand on his shoulder. Big Jim picked him up out of the water and shoved him toward the bank. In a few minutes the trapper had the pelts across his own back, dripping with water, twice as heavy as they were before. He splashed angrily through the stream to the shore.

He dumped the possible sack full of pelts on the ground and swore bitterly. Finally he faced the shivering boy.

The thundering voice roared, "Get out of my sight before I . . . Go on!"

Loma's teeth were chattering so that he couldn't talk. He turned and disappeared down the stream bank, leaving his snowshoes behind.

Big Jim shook out each pelt, repacked them, picked up the boy's snowshoes and started out for the last trap. "No-good Injun," he mumbled to himself as he shuffled along under the heavy pack. "I'd have been better off to have bought a mule."

When he arrived near the last trap, it was empty. It was easy to see that the trap had been sprung. He moved up closer. The trap had been pulled up on the bank, but there was no beaver leg. The beaver hadn't got away by chewing himself free. He noticed moccasin prints around the trap and smiled. "Looks like the little Injun wanted to make up for what he did by carrying the dead beaver back to the cabin for me." In better humor he reset the trap farther downstream. "Beaver couldn't have weighed much," he mused as he followed the small moccasin prints along the bank. "There're no signs of the boy's dragging it; must be carrying the thing. Too bad he didn't have a knife to skin it out. No, best that he didn't. Would have botched up that job."

Farther on he noticed that the moccasin prints sank deep into the snow. "That's what he gets for forgetting the snow-shoes. What a struggle he must be having." Big Jim laughed a little to himself that the boy was so determined to make up to him for what he hadn't been doing all day.

Loma cradled the beaver in his arms. He had found it still alive, his leg badly chewed and torn. At sight of the boy, the beaver had panicked, tried to duck away by diving deeper into the water. Loma pulled the trap up, the beaver still struggling to get away. The boy spoke to him in Hopi.

"I will not harm you, little beaver. Do not be afraid."

All the while he talked, he worked the mutilated leg free from the trap. Finally the beaver stopped struggling. He was still afraid, but he had used up all of his strength during the day trying to free himself of the trap. Loma started to put him back into the stream, then noticed that the beaver had so little strength he would drown. And the leg needed care in order to heal properly. In a soothing voice the boy told the beaver what he was going to do.

"I will carry you with me and take care of you until the leg is well. You can live in the shed with the horses, and I will gather aspen twigs for you to eat. The same life spirit that is in you is in me. For that reason you must know I wish you no harm."

As Loma lifted the body into his arms, the young beaver opened both eyes. The boy hummed a Hopi chant until the eyes closed, then he moved forward through the deep snow toward the cabin more than two miles away. The wet buckskin seemed to freeze against his skin. The air was cold. Loma shivered.

The young beaver was no heavier than ten pounds, but by the time Loma reached the shed he thought his arms would break under the weight. He laid the beaver in the feed room where the horses would not disturb him. Then he went out again and broke small aspen branches from the trees. These were laid close to the injured beaver. The boy filled one of the wooden water buckets with snow and set it beside the beaver's head in case he became thirsty during the night. He ran into the cabin, found the bottle of medicine Big Jim had brought in case he met with a mountain lion or a bear or some unforeseen injury that he said could happen to a man in the mountains.

Hurriedly Loma doctored the leg, covered it with moss, and wrapped it in a piece of soft buckskin. He hoped the beaver didn't decide to chew the bandage off. With such long teeth it looked to Loma as if the young beaver could chew anything. He gazed down at the helpless ball of fur and wondered if he would live until morning.

While Loma fed the horses he told them, "You have a new neighbor in there. Be kind to him for he is very sick." He ran to the cabin to remove his clothes before they froze his skin.

When Big Jim entered the front door the boy was wrapped in a buffalo robe standing in front of the fireplace stirring a pot of beans. The coffee was bubbling and strong the way Big Jim liked it. The man took a cup down from the cupboard and filled it with hot coffee, then he spread the red coals around in the fireplace and laid two beaver tails across the hot bed. He sat down near the fire to change his wet moccasins.

Loma's heart beat wildly. Had Big Jim seen the empty trap? Would Big Jim beat him with a trap chain as he said he might? Afraid to face the mountain man, he kept his back to him and stirred the beans quickly.

"Well, boy," Big Jim boomed in a pleasant voice. "Do you have something you want to tell me?"

Loma shook his head, no. It was true, he didn't want to tell about the beaver.

Big Jim grinned. "Don't be modest. When a man does something he's proud of, he should come out with it. I can tell you I'm mighty proud of the number of beaver I got me today. You can bet your moccasins I'm proud. And I sure ain't ashamed to admit it.''

Loma decided he wasn't proud of having saved the beaver; it was just something that had had to be done.

''Yessir, when a boy acts like a man by going out and doing something good on his own . . . well, by golly that's something to be proud of. You sure you ain't got something you want to tell me?''

Big Jim tried to act casual, but he was anxious to get a look at the beaver pelt.

Loma tapped the wooden spoon on the side of the iron kettle, then laid it on the stone hearth. He pulled the buffalo robe tighter around him and turned around.

Big Jim is smiling, he thought. Perhaps when an animal is injured as this beaver is injured, Big Jim is proud to see his life saved. The man has a good heart for animals after all. Loma's lips moved slowly into a half smile.

''I find beaver,'' Loma said shyly.

''Good boy. Where is it?''

''In shed. Horse shed.''

''The horse shed! Why'd you leave it out there? Well, that part isn't important, let's take a look.''

As the man and boy walked to the shed, Big Jim asked about the pelt. ''What kind of shape is it in?'' He tried to make his voice sound offhand.

Loma gazed up at him through the darkness. ''Not good,'' he said in a low voice. ''You help?''

''Yeah, I sure will, if you haven't ruined it completely.''

They walked into the shed, but it was too dark to see anything. Big Jim groped his way through the night trying to adjust his eyes. ''Where the devil is it?''

58

"Here," Loma answered, petting the horses as he walked by them to the feed room.

When they entered the small room, Loma knelt down beside the curled-up ball of fur. The beaver slapped his tail weakly against the ground.

The sound stopped Big Jim dead-still in his tracks. "It's alive!" he roared at the top of his lungs.

The horses jumped away nervously.

Loma nodded his head above the buffalo robe and gazed tenderly down at the young beaver.

Big Jim stood unbelieving, his mouth open in a state of shock.

Day after day Big Jim took Loma with him to the stream. Day after day the man's temper grew. He had paid out good money for a worthless boy. He had expected to teach the boy how to trap so he wouldn't have to do all the hard work himself. His plans were to send Loma out for a week upstream while he went downstream, allow for a few days' rest at the cabin, then both of them would travel separate ways again. By spring he hoped to have twice as many beaver pelts as he normally could have trapped by himself. Instead, the boy refused to set traps, refused to kill more beaver than they needed to eat, refused to hunt rabbits on the way just for the fun of it.

By the end of a week Big Jim was furious. He grabbed up his knife and marched out to the shed with full intentions of killing the beaver Loma had brought in. When he arrived, the boy was changing the beaver's bandage and doctoring the battered leg with the trapper's private medicine. Angrily, Big Jim knelt down to cut the beaver's throat. Loma looked

60

up at him with pleading eyes. Big Jim hesitated, glanced away from the boy's dark eyes, stuck the knife into his belt, and stomped out.

When Loma came back to the cabin, Big Jim was packing supplies. He closed the pack, slung it over his shoulder and walked moodily to the door. Without looking at Loma, he growled, "There's a man's work waiting to be done and I don't want any sissy kid tagging along. First thing when I get back to Santa Fe in the spring I'm going to sell you. It's a waste of money even to keep your belly full." He stomped out across the snow. Over his shoulder he called, "Three days I'll be gone. You better be here when I get back."

Loma watched him go. He wanted to be of help to Big Jim, but he could not bring himself to kill except for need. That was against everything he had been taught.

When Big Jim was out of sight Loma turned toward the shed. Inside the feed room the young beaver was busily nipping off tender twigs from the aspen branch Loma had given him hours before. The boy sat quietly and watched. After eating the twigs the beaver held the branch in his paws, turning it round and round as he nibbled off the bark. When the bark and sap were gone, he picked up another twig.

Satisfied with his meal the beaver sat up to comb himself. Balancing on his flat tail, he groomed his coat with his uninjured hind foot. Loma noticed that the little beaver had a split claw on each hind foot, perfect for combing his fur.

The beaver was used to having the boy with him. Not once did he try to bite when Loma doctored the leg and often the beaver would talk to him in a squeaky voice.

On the third night of Big Jim's departure, as Loma was sitting in front of the fireplace thinking of the other captured children, a knock sounded on the cabin door. Fearfully,

Loma looked around. It came again, followed by a weak voice.

The boy rose, walked silently across the room and opened the door. An old Indian stumbled in. Loma stared at him. The old man was dressed much like his own people, yet there was something about him that told Loma the Indian was not Hopi.

The old Indian, half-starved and cold, stumbled toward the fire. After warming himself he turned to the boy. "You are here alone?" the old man asked in his own language.

Loma nodded. Although the language was not his, he could understand it. "The man who owns me is away trapping," he answered.

The old man's eyes brightened. "You are Hopi."

"Yes." Loma took a tin plate from the cupboard and heaped it high with food.

"You are very kind," the old Indian said, eating the food quickly with his fingers. He nodded when Loma refilled the plate. "I have not eaten in three days. Thank you."

After finishing the second helping of food, the old Indian set the plate aside and cleaned each finger by sticking it in his mouth. Huddled near the fireplace, he said to Loma, "You are one of the stolen children?"

Loma nodded.

"I have left Santa Fe only four days ago for my pueblo in Taos."

Loma smiled. "I have heard my people speak of Taos. Your way is the Hopi way."

"Yes. My people are related to your people."

"How do you know about me?" Loma asked.

The old man's words could scarcely be heard, they were spoken so gently and so low. "News of the captured children has spread like the wind to the four directions."

62

Somehow the old man's gentle words helped Loma to feel less lonely. The words made him feel closer to his mother and father than he had for some time. "Do you have news of my people?" Loma asked.

"Yes. But it is not good news. Two men of the Badger Clan from your village in Oraibi tried to make the trip to Santa Fe. It was their plan to bring Wickvaya's young wife and the children back to their homes. Because of the warring tribes who do not mind killing Hopi, it was decided that the men must travel at night. But in three days they returned to Oraibi because the warring tribes threatened them at all times. I know this is true," the old man said quietly. "My Navajo friend told me his brother was with the riders who chased the Hopi men."

"I do not like the Navajos," Loma said flatly.

The old man smiled upon the boy. "Not all Navajo are bad, just as not all Hopi are good. We are given life upon Mother Earth to learn. There are some who must learn more than others. But the journey of learning is as long as the journey of life."

Loma was quiet a moment, thinking about the old man's words. "I wonder," he said thoughtfully, "if the people of my village will try again to find us?"

The Taos Indian shook his head slowly. "My mind does not know, but my heart tells me they will." His dark eyes closed for a moment.

The boy sat very still, then leaned forward and lightly touched the old man on the shoulder. "Will you rest here tonight?" he asked kindly.

The old eyes opened, deep quiet pools filled with peace. "Thank you."

Loma handed him the heavy buffalo robe. "You will need this when the fire dies before morning."

The old man shook his head, but Loma insisted. He placed two small logs on the fire, then wrapped up in a wool blanket and lay down on the far side of the fireplace across from the old Indian.

Just before dropping off to sleep Loma opened his eyes to see if the old man was comfortable. The Taos Indian was sitting cross-legged deep in meditation. Loma knew it by the look of timelessness on the old man's face, and the way his wrinkled hands lay folded peacefully in his lap.

And through the power of the old Indian's thoughts, Loma felt himself being lifted upward, higher and higher on the wings of an eagle into the beauty beyond this world.

During the sunrise, while the old Indian slept, Loma tiptoed out of the cabin. Once inside the shed, he told the horses of the visitor who had stopped by on his way to Taos. The horses followed him to the feedbox, nuzzled him on the back as he walked and nickered low, happy to see their friend. While the horses were eating, the boy went into the feed room to doctor the young beaver. The little brown eyes blinked and the flat tail smacked against the ground. Then the beaver stood up on his haunches and made the squeaking noise that Loma liked to hear.

"You are better today," he said happily. "I think your leg will heal now without the protection of the buckskin covering. Hold still while I put on the medicine."

The beaver chattered eagerly while Loma worked on his leg. "The chirping of hungry birds comes from your throat. A wise beaver would wait patiently for his breakfast."

In answer the flat tail banged noisily against the hard ground. Loma laughed, picked up the hatchet, and started out of the shed to cut aspen branches for the hungry beaver.

He climbed higher up the tree than usual hoping to see Big Jim returning from the trapping trip. Loma was sorry the man had been angry when he left, but even in his anger he had said he would be gone only three days. Today was the fourth day and Big Jim was nowhere in sight. When Loma was high in the tree, he chopped the tender branches and let them fall to the snow-covered ground beneath. As he was sliding down the white aspen trunk he saw the old Indian walk out of the cabin, the heavy blanket wrapped tightly around him. First, the old man turned to the sun and stood for a few moments in meditation, then he followed the narrow path to the shed.

Loma hurriedly gathered the fallen branches and dragged them to the shed where the old man stood stroking one of the horses with a work-gnarled hand.

"The boy of no name is an early riser."

"I am called Loma," he said smiling.

"And I am called Tall Walking Rain," the old man smiled back. He took one of the larger aspen branches and followed Loma into the feed room.

The beaver hurriedly burrowed his way into the hay. Soon two bright brown eyes peeked through the hay at the stranger.

"He is not used to people," Loma explained.

The old Indian said nothing. He sat quietly, not a muscle moving, waiting for the beaver to come out.

"Do not be afraid," Loma cooed to the frightened beaver. "Tall Walking Rain is our friend."

After some minutes the beaver emerged, pieces of hay still on his back. Driven by hunger, he stuffed the bark into his mouth with both front paws, never taking his eyes from the strange man. Loma ran his hand over the furry back to remove the hay.

"He was caught in the trap, but his leg is almost well now. I think if he is strong enough to run and hide that he is ready to be put back in the stream. I am sure he misses his home."

The old man did not answer. He did not move. Only if he stayed quiet would the beaver allow the boy to doctor his leg. When Loma had finished, the old man rose from his sitting position. Again the beaver scurried in the hay to hide.

Tall Walking Rain placed his arm over Loma's shoulders. "Come, we will leave him in peace." As they moved through the shed, the old man said, "The horses are well cared for." It was not a compliment. He merely stated a fact.

Loma was pleased. Big Jim had never noticed. Suddenly the young beaver came to mind again. "If I put him back in the stream, how do I know Big Jim will not trap him?"

"Big Jim is the trapper who is away?"

"Yes."

"Put the beaver in the stream where you found him. That is his home. If the man has laid his traps around the dam where your beaver lives, then he will not go back there to lay traps again this winter."

"Are you sure?" Loma asked anxiously.

"No. I am not sure. But if the trapper believes he has caught all of the beaver he can from the one place, he will move his traps to other dams."

What the old man said was true. Big Jim trapped out one area completely, then moved his equipment to another area usually some miles up or down the stream.

After a long silence Loma said, "I will take the beaver to his home before the sun is high in the sky. It is not many miles; perhaps Tall Walking Rain would like to come."

The old man smiled. "Thank you," he said, "but the legs of an old man need rest. Many miles must my moccasins travel to reach Taos."

Loma and the old man ate breakfast in silence, a comfortable silence shared between friends.

While the old Indian smoked Loma straightened up the cabin. Then he slipped the bear skin over his head and went to Tall Walking Rain. "I will take the beaver now. Will you rest here today?"

"The man you call Big Jim, when does he return?"

"I do not know." Worry sounded in Loma's voice. "He was to be away three days. Today is the fourth day."

"There are some trappers," the old man said slowly, "who will shoot an Indian on sight. If he should come while you are away my spirit might be freed from this body. It is not yet time for my death. There is yet work to be done."

"I do not believe Big Jim kills Indians." He smiled. "He has not killed me."

The old man nodded. "That is because you are his slave. Take your beaver and do not worry. I shall be here when you return."

Loma hurried out of the cabin to the shed. He thought of taking a horse. It would be easier to hold the beaver across the withers than in his arms. Then he put the thought away. A ride on the horse would frighten the injured beaver and he did not want that. When he walked inside the feed room the young beaver was busily gnawing the bark of a limb down to the sweet sap. He looked up at the boy, then went back to the branch.

"Come, my friend. Today you must return to your home. It is better that you are gone from here when Big Jim arrives. The life in you disturbs him."

Loma lifted the ball of fur into his arms, walked out past the curious horses, into the open air. He held the struggling beaver in one arm while putting on the snowshoes. After what seemed a very long time he finally had the big shoes in place, stood up and shuffled over the snow toward the stream.

The air was chill and the snow glistened in the sun. Big chunks of snow dropped from the spruce and pine trees making holes in the snow crust beneath. In the distance Loma saw a deer. It stood for a moment staring at the boy and the beaver. Suddenly it turned to run. No sound could be heard beneath the fleet foot of the deer. As quickly as the deer had run, it stopped, stared again at the boy and the beaver, then again ran, out of sight.

In less than an hour Loma reached the stream. The beaver chattered excitedly as they neared the mud and stick dam. Loma knelt at the side of the stream, close to the place he had found the injured beaver, and with some regret at losing his friend, released the squirming ball of fur. The beaver dived headlong into the water. After a short time he reappeared, blinked his round brown eyes at the boy on the stream bank as if to say goodbye, then disappeared.

"It is good that you are happy," said the boy. "I hope some of your family are left to welcome you."

As he turned to leave, he noticed the tracks of his snowshoes. If Big Jim should see them he would know exactly where the young beaver had been returned to the water. Loma broke a spruce branch from a nearby tree and carefully retraced his steps, sweeping the snowshoe tracks away. He felt a little guilty for having deceived Big Jim, but the guilt was not as strong as knowing he had done the right thing. The beaver was now free to follow his own trail of life.

Slowly happiness filled his body. He lifted his eyes from the snow below him, tossed the spruce branch away and ran the best he could on the clumsy snowshoes all the way back to the cabin.

The boy half expected to find Big Jim waiting. But there was only Tall Walking Rain sitting next to the fire, his thoughts turned inward, closing his mind to the world around him. Loma slipped the heavy bearskin off over his head, then sat down to remove the snowshoes. He tried to be very quiet, but his presence in the room was felt by the old man who turned to him.

"The beaver is home safely?"

"Yes."

The old man looked steadily at the boy. "Soon I must leave for my pueblo in Taos. Does the young Hopi wish to travel with Tall Walking Rain?"

Loma's heart skipped a beat. If he left with the old man, he would be free, no longer the slave to Big Jim. The people of Taos would see that he was returned to his own people where he belonged. Then a shadow came creeping over his thoughts. What about Big Jim? Could he leave the cabin not knowing if the rough mountain man was all right? Loma scolded himself. What did he care if the trapper was all right or not? He didn't care . . . yet he did. But why? There was no reason for him to care, he was only a slave. Or was he more than that? Big Jim could have bought other boys older than himself who would have been more help. He could have hired a man who knew about trapping, rather than a Hopi who did not believe in killing. Josie was half Tewa Indian. Big Jim must have known that Hopis did not believe in killing for money . . . Loma cupped his chin in his hands. Why had Big Jim bought him in the first place?

"The heart of a boy is troubled," said the old Indian kindly.

Loma nodded, not wanting to look up.

"You, my son," said the old man slowly, "are an old soul and if you listen to your intuition you will know that the man who is called Big Jim has need of your assistance."

The boy lifted his dark eyes and gazed into the face of wisdom. He listened to the voice that seemed to come from somewhere beyond the old man himself.

"Through all life will run the one great truth: the merging of each individual life into the one great life and while we are following the road to the one great truth, each of us has a duty to himself and to others. It is a difficult task to know where our duty lies."

Loma's words were loud and quick. "My duty does not lie with Big Jim!"

The old man nodded. "Only you can know."

For a long time the boy sat in silence. His thoughts rushed like the waters of a swift-flowing stream. Time passed. The old man waited patiently for the boy to know what was right.

Finally the storm in the boy's mind subsided. He hung his head as he groped for an answer. Then, in a weak voice he said, "I feel in my heart that something is wrong. I must look for Big Jim."

The old man said nothing. Only his eyes showed approval.

7 Early the next morning Loma bent over the sleeping Indian. "I must go now," he said softly.

The old man turned in his blanket. "Saddle two horses. I will fix the food we need."

"We?" Loma questioned.

"The young hawk wishes to fly alone?"

"No. Only I thought . . ."

"The wind covers tracks with snow. The sun melts prints so the eye cannot see. An inexperienced nose cannot smell a fire miles away. A boy's memory of a trail once taken can grow dim. I know these mountains. I have traveled them from my pueblo in Taos to Santa Fe and from Santa Fe back to my pueblo in Taos. Many times I have stopped at this cabin to rest with Beaver Charlie."

Loma was shocked. "You had not eaten in three days. You were cold and hungry. I thought you were lost."

"No, not lost. Outside of Santa Fe a small band of raiders stole my food and my heavy blanket. I travel night and day by the way the eagle flies to cabin where I expect to find Beaver Charlie. But I find a boy instead. The boy is good. He feeds me and invites me to rest. Now I will repay your kindness.''

Happily, Loma saddled the horses. The old Indian brought a small bundle of food into the shed, tied it on the back of one saddle, then picked up the hatchet and tied that on the other saddle. Without a word he led the horse out of the shed and mounted. Loma followed.

They rode all morning in silence, and Loma marveled at the old man's knowledge. Not once did he guide the horse into a deep snowdrift. He seemed to know inwardly where the high ground lay. He kept a steady pace that did not tire the horses and sat straight in the saddle with no noticeable movement. Now and then the old Indian pointed to a broken twig jutting out of a tree and Loma would know Big Jim had been by that way.

Only once during the day did the old Indian slow down and that was to give Loma two corn cakes. Loma was grateful. For a long while his stomach had been churning from hunger.

Later, as the sun neared the western horizon and the shadows lengthened across the dull white snow, the old man reined his horse to a stop. "It is the time when the sun must go to the underworld. Soon the night will throw its blanket across the mountains and the moon of lesser light will smile down upon the earth.''

Loma waited quietly for the old Indian to continue.

"We must stop for the night and let the horses eat what grass they are able to paw up from under the snow. They have carried us well.''

Loma nodded. They unsaddled the horses and Tall Walking Rain fastened a rawhide strap around each horse's hind legs. Loma watched him, puzzled.

The old man straightened up. "The hobbles on the horses' hind legs will allow their front legs freedom to paw in the snow for the grass underneath. At the same time they will keep the hind legs close together so the horses will not wander away during the night."

Loma gathered wood for the fire while the old man fed the tiny flame with small twigs. As they ate a meager meal Loma gazed into the night, his eyes fixed on the one revealed star overhead. He wondered why some stars came out earlier than others.

"Perhaps tomorrow we shall find your friend," said the old man.

Loma lowered his dark eyes to the fire. "Big Jim is not my friend," he said.

The old man looked knowingly at the boy. "You speak in haste. Your thoughts run wildly only to crash into the underbrush. The wise man controls his mind as his hand upon the rein controls the horse. One must listen to the heart before the tongue moves."

Loma was irritated. The old man seemed to have an answer for everything. Deliberately he said, "Killing is his way of life. It is not the Hopi way. Perhaps you think it is all right."

Loma was ashamed. He had spoken sharp words to the kind old man. One part of him was sorry for what he had said, but still, as he watched Tall Walking Rain sleeping in peace, he thought, Big Jim was *not* his friend! Then he too slept.

By the time Loma awoke next morning, warm and snug in the buffalo robe, the old man had the horses saddled ready to continue their search for Big Jim.

After a light breakfast, Loma felt better. He rode the horse behind the old Indian, confident that this day they would find the trapper. When the sun was high in the clear sky, Tall Walking Rain reined in his horse. He stretched a long arm forward and pointed at a large beaver dam in the distance.

"Do you think he is there?" Loma asked, trying not to show his excitement.

"It is difficult to tell. The trail is three days old. He might have journeyed on after setting some of the traps here. We shall see."

They rode closer to the large mud and stick dam. Loma strained his dark eyes to search the pond behind the dam. Suddenly he stood up in the stirrups. "Look! I see a beaver trap."

The old man nodded, kicked his horse forward and dismounted on the bank near the trap. With some effort he pulled the trap out of the water. In it was a dead beaver. Without a word he placed the beaver on the ground, mounted and followed the stream bank north.

The man and boy rode for thirty minutes before another beaver trap was spotted. It too held a dead beaver weighing nearly sixty pounds. "I am puzzled," said the old Indian. "The beaver have been dead two days at least. If Big Jim was to be gone only three days, he would have picked them up by now."

"Listen," whispered Loma.

There was only silence, but something told the old Indian that the boy was right. A strangeness filled the silence. He handed the reins of his horse to Loma and walked a few yards away to listen. Then he turned away from the stream to the forest trees. In a few minutes he reappeared and motioned the boy to follow.

There, lying in the snow beneath a tall spruce tree, was Big Jim. The fear that showed in Loma's eyes told Tall Walking Rain his thoughts.

"No," said the old man gently, "he is not dead. But he is close to it."

"What happened?" Loma asked, jumping down from the horse.

The old Indian shook his head. "I do not know. The leg is broken. You see." He slit the buckskin pantleg with Big Jim's sharp knife.

Loma's face paled. Two jagged bones stuck out from a large hole torn in the skin. He looked away from Big Jim's leg to his face, which was almost white beneath the reddish-yellow beard. His lips seemed a light blue color. "Does he have frostbite?" Loma asked the last two words in English.

"I see he has been teaching you his language. Yes, he has frostbite. I hope he does not lose part of his face."

Loma gasped.

"Be glad he is still alive. It is a wonder he has not taken the sleep of the snow never to wake to this life again. Now, I must mend the bones."

Loma watched the old man skillfully cut and skin small aspen branches. Then he cut the rest of the pantleg off of Big Jim.

"Bring me the bag on my saddle," he told Loma.

As the boy hurried to the horse he heard a muffled scream. He leaned against the horse for a moment, then ran back to the old man and Big Jim. When he brought himself to look again at the leg, the bones were together, no longer sticking out of the skin. He handed Tall Walking Rain the bag, then stood back and watched while the old man splinted the leg. The old Indian moved to Big Jim's head and poured some liquid into his mouth. The mountain man swallowed, tried to open his eyes, then lay back in the snow. Only his lips moved. "I'm tired of dying . . ." he whispered hoarsely.

The old man poured more liquid into Big Jim's mouth, then moved quietly away with the knife and the hatchet. "Spread the buffalo robe out on the snow, skin side down," he instructed.

The boy did as he was told. Soon Tall Walking Rain reappeared with two long poles, which he had chopped from the trunks of young aspen trees. He made holes in the buffalo robe, then with rawhide thongs he attached the robe to the poles. Loma realized the old man was making a cradle to carry Big Jim.

"The trip back will not be easy," he told the boy. "We will attach the poles to the saddle and drag your friend in the travois behind the horse. The horse must work hard, for the snow is deep and the poles will sink in. Now we must carry the mountain man over and lay him on the buffalo robe between the poles. Bring the horse as close to him as you can."

Loma obeyed. The horse looked questioningly as the travois was attached to his saddle. His back humped. Loma talked to him in a soft voice. Finally the hump left his back and the old Indian went to the injured man, and told Loma what to do next.

"Reach under his arm at the shoulder. Good. I will do the same with the other arm. We will drag him up on the buffalo robe behind the horse."

As they lifted Big Jim's torso from the ground, a moan of pain escaped the injured man.

"Do not stop," insisted the old Indian. "Some of his ribs are also broken, but we must get him on the travois."

Loma bit his lip as they moved the big man a few inches at a time over the snow up the buffalo hide that held firmly between the two poles. Perspiration broke out on the old man and the boy. Steadily they pulled until Big Jim's head was up close to the horse's tail.

"Good," said Tall Walking Rain. He folded the extra part of the robe over the unconscious man and tied him in the sling. "We will go."

"What about the beaver?" Loma asked. "Big Jim will want their pelts."

The old man smiled to himself. The boy who hated Big Jim's way of life was ready to protect his interests. "They are too heavy to carry unless they are skinned. We must not wait any longer."

Loma looked at Big Jim. Finally he said, "I will skin the beavers and catch up with you."

Tall Walking Rain nodded. "You need a horse to carry the pelts and the traps. Hurry. You must catch up with us before the sun puts the day away."

Hesitantly Loma accepted the skinning knife, stuck it in his belt, took the reins of the horse and started toward the stream.

Before dark the boy had found and skinned five beaver. It was a distasteful job. Loma threw the innards into the stream to feed the fish, but he saved the tails to roast over hot coals for Big Jim. He was sorry the beavers were dead. At the same time he was grateful none of them were still alive in the traps. He didn't know how he would be able to carry a wounded beaver on the horse with the pelts and traps all the way back to the cabin. He scolded himself for thinking such thoughts, tied the last beaver pelt behind the saddle, lugged the trap up with the others and mounted.

In a few minutes the sun dipped behind the mountains. Loma urged the horse into a fast walk. He wanted to catch up with the old man and Big Jim as soon after dark as he could.

When he found them, Big Jim was semi-conscious, mumbling incoherently. Loma rode up beside the old Indian. "What is Big Jim saying?"

"Big Jim is saying nothing," the old Indian said. "It is the fever talking."

"Will he be all right?"

"The fever will keep him warm. That is good. I do not know if he will be all right. The leg is very bad. The ribs make it difficult for him to breathe. I think, if you do not mind, that we will ride all night."

Loma nodded. "When the sun smiles again we should be at the cabin?"

"Yes. It is better that the big man does not spend another night on the cold ground."

They lapsed into silence. As they rode slowly through the dark mountains, Loma was suddenly very grateful to the old man. If Tall Walking Rain had not come with him, what would he have done? Big Jim could not move himself and he was much too heavy for Loma to move alone. I would not have known how to make the cradle, he thought. If it were not for the wise old man, Big Jim would have died.

Later that night it began to snow, a soft gentle snow that

reminded Loma of a night when he and his father had climbed out of the kiva. Fresh snow had landed on his face, cooling it from the heat of the underground chamber. He and his father had gone to the house for Loma's mother. The three of them had walked slowly to the edge of the mesa and stood looking out into the vast night. They had done it for no reason except that they had wanted to. The memory of that night warmed Loma as he rode beside Tall Walking Rain.

"Take my blanket," said the old Indian, "and place it over your friend. It is not good that he should be cold during the night."

Loma shook his head. Why was the old man forever calling Big Jim his friend? "He shall have this bearskin. I do not like it anyway." He got off the horse, pulled the bearskin over his head and walked back to the feverish man. Gently he tucked the bearskin around Big Jim. He pulled it up to the big man's chin, then pulled the beaverskin hat down to his nose. "It will keep the snow from your face and still let you breathe," he explained.

"He does not understand what you are saying. Come."

The rest of the night Loma slapped his arms against his chest and hunched his shoulders. The buckskin shirt and pants did little to keep the cold away from his body. But it was better than traveling tied to a Spanish soldier, with bare feet and his cotton clothing. He would not complain.

Loma thought the night would never end. He glanced back frequently at Big Jim who sometimes babbled feverish words and sometimes lay completely still. Tall Walking Rain said nothing, but Loma could feel his uneasiness. Finally the old man spoke.

"Soon the gray dawn will spread over these mountains. We will arrive at the cabin before the new day is born. You ride ahead and ready the fire. Do you know the trail?

Loma peered through the darkness. "I think I can find it," he said.

"Good. Do not change directions until the dawn lights your way. Then you will know where you are."

Loma squeezed his legs into the horse's sides. The horse moved forward leaving the slower horse and his burden behind. When it was light enough to see, Loma knew exactly where he was, just as the old man had said.

The horses nickered loudly as Loma and his mount neared the shed. They had eaten the extra supply of hay that Loma had thrown out to them and they were hungry. He hurriedly unsaddled his horse, fed them all, and brushed the saddle marks from the horse's warm back. He placed the beaver pelts to dry as Big Jim had taught him, then ran to the cabin to build a fire and eat something himself. Tall Walking Rain didn't have much of an appetite and Loma had been hungry since they left. He dished himself a bowl full of ice-cold leftover stew and ate while he built the fire. His hands could hardly grasp the bowl, he was so cold.

Gradually the cabin chill was replaced by a warm glow. Loma made coffee and set the pot in the fire for the old man. Suddenly he remembered the beaver tails. He ran to the shed, grabbed one of the tails and hurried back to the warm cabin.

By the time Tall Walking Rain arrived with Big Jim, the beaver tail was cooked, ready to eat. The old man rode the horse up close to the cabin door. He untied the poles from the saddle and with Loma's help, moved them around until they were inside the cabin. Then the two of them slid the badly worn buffalo robe across the floor near the fireplace.

"I will take care of the horse," Loma suggested.

"Thank you, " the old man said as he knelt to untie Big Jim from the homemade stretcher.

When Loma returned to the cabin the old Indian was stretching the buckskin shirt tight across Big Jim's chest and stomach. "Does this man have a large piece of buckskin which he uses for mending?" Tall Walking Rain asked.

Loma nodded, unwrapped a bundle of odds and ends, took out a long strip of buckskin and handed it to the old Indian.

"Good. It is big enough to go around him."

The old man worked quickly. Loma watched him take the buckskin under Big Jim. The trapper groaned. A few minutes later the buckskin strap was in place, tied tightly around the broken ribs.

"The pain will now be less when he breathes." said the old man, straightening up. "While I fix his leg, you make some cornmeal mush. It is a long time since Big Jim eats. He will be hungry when the fever leaves."

Loma filled the iron pot with snow which he melted over the fire. When the water was boiling, he sprinkled in the cornmeal. All the while Tall Walking Rain worked over the leg, Loma concentrated on stirring the cornmeal. He could not bring himself to look again at the wound.

Finally the old man folded his blanket and sat down cross-legged on the floor. Loma handed him a cup of hot coffee. "Ahhh," he said drinking the coffee. "It is good to be warm."

Loma cut the beaver tail in two, gave the old man the larger half and sat down. A worried expression crossed his dark eyes as he glanced at Big Jim.

The old man noticed. In a kind voice he said, "Eat. We must wait. That is all there is left for us to do."

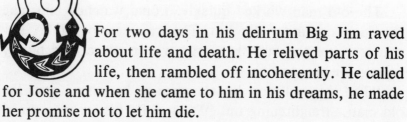

For two days in his delirium Big Jim raved about life and death. He relived parts of his life, then rambled off incoherently. He called for Josie and when she came to him in his dreams, he made her promise not to let him die.

Loma and the old man sat quietly. Loma tried to close his ears to the raving man, but he could not. It seemed to him that at times Tall Walking Rain turned his thoughts inward, not hearing the feverish trapper at all. When that happened Loma would go outside and breathe the fresh mountain air.

On the morning of the third day, the fever broke. Tall Walking Rain spooned warm mush into the mountain man's mouth. Afterward, Big Jim slept peacefully.

"It is strange," said the old Indian in a soft voice, "how a man who hunts the life of others is afraid to die."

Loma looked up startled. The words were his own thoughts. "Why is it?" he asked.

The old man shook his head. "I do not know. The most violent men are the most afraid. Perhaps it is because they do not understand life that they are so afraid of death."

Together the old Indian and the boy went to the shed to feed the horses. Afterward they walked through the snow going no place in particular. "You are not afraid of death," the boy said.

The old Indian smiled down at him. "What is death but new life?"

"My father has said that life and death are like the rising and setting sun. But I do not remember how."

"Then I will tell you. Before the sunrise comes the blue dawn, which signifies the breath of awakening. Soon the yellow breath turns into brilliant red, the reflection of the sun fire, the sign of manifested life. Gradually, the proud color disappears as the sun gives full light to a new day."

Loma listened closely. It was as if his own father were talking. The old Indian went on.

"It is like the rising sun that a new child is born into this world. At the time of the child's birth, he takes his first breath of this life. His body is red for awhile, then fades and the natural color of the skin is seen. As the child grows older, he gives life to other children of his own. He works with sun and the earth in harmony to grow food and to learn to use the gifts of nature for good."

"Then the daylight of people and the daylight of the sun are the same?"

The old man nodded. "Yes. And just as the sun does, when a man has done his work here on earth, he slips into the other world to rest for awhile. If he has been good, he leaves beautiful thoughts that reach out across the earth and sky. These thoughts are his sunset to remind people of the pattern of Creation and of the harmony in nature."

"Your words are much like the words of my father."

"Words of truth belong to all people."

"Truth is a word I think I do not understand."

"Truth," said the old man in a faraway voice, "is a bright star dropped from the heart of eternity."

Loma thought about it. He might not understand the exact meaning of the words, but something about the tone of the old man's voice filled Loma with a good feeling. It was enough.

When they arrived again at the cabin, Big Jim was awake. He turned his head toward them. "I'm dry as the bleached bones of the dead. I need water."

The old man smiled at the boy. "He is going to be all right."

Big Jim tried to raise himself up on one elbow. A flash of pain crossed his face. Quickly he lay back down. The old Indian held the trapper's head up off the buffalo robe while he drank the water. Satisfied, Big Jim lay back and looked straight at Tall Walking Rain.

"Who are you?"

"I am an old man journeying across the mountains to my pueblo in Taos."

Surprise showed in Loma's face. "You did not tell me you spoke English," he said.

"You did not ask," the old man said gently.

Loma moved up beside Big Jim. "He is called Tall Walking Rain," he explained in English.

"Tall Walking Rain, huh? You the one Beaver Charlie's always talking about?" His voice was thin and shallow, not the thunderous roar that Loma was used to hearing.

"Beaver Charlie and I are friends. I do not know if he talks of me."

Big Jim looked from the old man to the boy. He gazed around the cabin. "How'd I get here?"

The old Indian answered. "Loma saved your life."

Big Jim's eyes rested again on the boy. "I thought you'd be long gone. Figured you for a deserter."

"The boy is no deserter. I offered to take him with me to Taos where he would be free to return to his own people. He refused to leave you."

Big Jim frowned. "Don't feed me none of your bull, Injun."

"It is true. Because of the boy we rode out to find you. When you did not return in three days, the boy was afraid something had happened. How else could we have found you and brought you here?"

Big Jim looked at the boy as if seeing him for the first time. "Well, I'll be," he whispered to himself. Then quickly he added, "'Course that doesn't change the fact that he's got no nerve. Can't even kill a beaver or skin out a hide."

In a stern voice the old man said, "Does it take nerve to set a beaver trap? Does it take nerve to skin the beaver once he is dead? Listen to me, mountain man. This boy made the journey to the salt caves in Grand Canyon last year when he was only ten years old. It is a journey even grown men fear because of its dangers. Loma is not a hawk too weak to fly, he is an eagle, brave enough to live the way his heart tells him is right."

Big Jim was not used to being lectured. His temper flared. He tried to shout at the quiet-spoken Indian, but it hurt him to talk above a hoarse whisper. "If he's so doggone brave, why couldn't he learn to kill a lousy beaver?"

"He has no reason to kill."

"Money's reason enough."

"For you perhaps. Not for him. The beaver has as much right to follow his journey through life as you or I."

"Rot!"

Ignoring this, the old man continued. "The boy gathered and skinned the five beaver where we found you. The pelts are drying in the shed."

Amazement crossed the trapper's pale face.

"Yes, mountain man. I was willing to leave the beaver behind, but Loma would not. He knew you would want them."

"You're telling me the truth?"

"You know that."

Big Jim relaxed. "So you finally learned your lesson. That's good. While I'm laid up you can set traps for me."

"No," said the old man flatly.

Big Jim turned angrily. Pain shot through his chest. His breath came in short gasps. He waited until the pain passed, then, "If I wasn't busted up, I'd . . . Who do you think you are? He's my slave!"

"I have told you," said the old Indian calmly. "It is not our way of life to kill except for need. Would you have him do what is wrong?"

"I *need* those pelts!" he demanded weakly.

"Then it is your duty to get them. It is not the duty of the boy."

"He's my slave!"

"He is your friend."

Big Jim sank back defeated. There was no arguing with the stubborn old man. Friend! He had no friends, except maybe Josie. Cautiously, out of the corner of his eye, he looked at the boy who sat beside him. For a moment he studied the grave dark eyes, then looked quickly away.

"Perhaps," said the old Indian, "you will tell us of your accident."

Big Jim blinked his eyes to shut off the thoughts going on in his mind. He turned his head slightly to the side. "Huh? Oh . . . yeah . . . my accident. Let's see, it was on the second day out . . . I was crossing the high falls to the other side of the stream when I spied a buck deer, one of the biggest spread of antlers I've ever seen. They would've made a fine trophy. I steadied myself on a rock. Wasn't easy, the water was swift . . . then I aimed my gun and . . . I . . . I don't know what happened. Maybe it backfired. Anyhow it knocked my feet plumb out from under me . . . The next thing I remember was crashing against the rocks at the bottom of the waterfall . . . I knew my leg was busted bad, but I managed to pull myself out of the stream to shore. Couldn't stay there . . . would have froze to death. Dragged myself under a tree and lit me a fire. Took a long time . . . I . . . I think I must've passed out once or twice doing it. Had a hard time breathing. Somehow kept the fire going during the night . . . it's all kind of hazy . . . Next morning . . . the big buck . . . was standing close by . . . saw his eyes . . . soft . . . beautiful . . . glad I hadn't shot . . ."

Big Jim's eyes closed. His mouth sagged open and he was quiet.

Loma lifted his dark eyes to Tall Walking Rain. "What is wrong?" he asked, frightened.

"Too much talk. It is better that he sleep," he answered in language Loma understood.

"He told you of the accident?" asked the boy.

The old man nodded, rose from the floor and walked slowly across the room to pour himself a cup of hot coffee.

"I do not understand English very well. What did he say?"

Tall Walking Rain repeated Big Jim's story.

Loma leaned forward. "What else did he say about the big deer?"

"That is all. He fell asleep."

Loma sat quietly for a few minutes, then, "I did not know Big Jim could like the eyes of a deer."

The old man smiled. "There is good in a man who sees beauty in the eyes of a deer."

Loma looked again at Big Jim lying helpless on the buffalo robe. Finally he said, "He does not like me."

"No," explained the old Indian. "It is not you that he does not like. It is the part of you he sees in himself that he does not understand."

Loma looked up puzzled.

"None of us like what we do not understand," the old man said.

"Perhaps," said Loma hopefully, "you will tell me what you mean."

The old Indian smiled. "You think. The answer is in you." He finished the coffee, set the cup on the floor and motioned Loma to him. "I must leave. My people are expecting me. While Big Jim sleeps I will show you how to prepare the poultice for his leg. Come."

Loma watched carefully as Tall Walking Rain took bits of plants and dried leaves and aspen ashes from his small pouch, mixed them together with a few drops of liquid, then patted them gently on the wound.

"Do this each morning and each night until the injury heals from the inside out."

A worried expression crossed Loma's face. "What if it becomes infected?"

"There will be no infection if you do as I say."

As Tall Walking Rain wrapped the buckskin bandage around the leg, Big Jim stirred. "I can't breathe," he whispered in panic.

The old Indian turned to him. "Your ribs are broken. Lie still and they will heal. The boy will take care of you."

Sudden fear showed in Big Jim's bearded face. "Where are you going?"

"To my pueblo in Taos."

"You can't," he whispered. "I'll die!"

"The boy will be here."

Big Jim started to object and fell back gasping. When he regained his breath he said, "The boy doesn't know about doctoring."

"I have given him instructions. He will care for you."

"What if the boy runs off?"

"He could have gone with me. He chose to stay. Remember, mountain man, Loma is the one who saved your life before. He will not let you die."

The old man rose, picked up the heavy cotton blanket and wrapped it around him. Loma packed enough food in a bag to last the old man until he reached Taos. Together they walked to the door.

"Wait! Don't go!" Big Jim called in a raspy voice.

Tall Walking Rain turned. "Goodbye, my friend," was all he said.

Once outside in the snow the Indian placed his hand on Loma's shoulder. "The thoughts of an old man will be with you."

Loma dug the toe of his moccasin in the snow. "Will you . . .," he said shyly, "take one of the horses? The journey will be easier."

"Thank you, but the horses are not yours to give."

"Boy!" called a heavy voice from the cabin.

Loma ran inside. Big Jim was breathing heavily from the exertion of the call. "Boy," he whispered. "Give the old man a horse. I won't be needing them all."

Loma grinned happily and raced outside. "The horse is yours," he said, catching up to Tall Walking Rain.

The old Indian smiled. "Your friend is kind. Tell him I will return the horse to Santa Fe when the snow melts."

"I think he does not want the horse. He said to give it to you."

Loma hurried to the shed, threw a saddle on one of the pack horses and was tightening the cinch when the old man walked in. "No saddle," he said. "No bridle. Only the horse."

"But how will you guide him?"

"A horse can be talked to with the hands and the legs. He will understand which way I wish to go."

Loma started to object, but it was too late. Tall Walking Rain removed the saddle, leaped on the horse's broad back and guided him with the pressure of his knees out of the shed.

A few yards away the old man stopped his horse, looked back over his shoulder and spoke in an even voice. "You are a good Hopi."

Loma watched him ride out of sight, then turned and walked slowly into the cabin.

For a long time Big Jim slept. When he finally woke, Loma was sitting cross-legged carving on a long narrow tree branch.

"What's that you're doing?" Big Jim demanded in a hoarse whisper.

Loma did not know how to say bow and arrow in English. He stood up, held the long branch in his hand and pulled back on an imaginary bowstring.

"Making a bow and arrows?"

Loma nodded.

"For what?"

In Hopi Loma said, "We have no meat. I will find a deer and explain to him your need. He will then willingly give up his earthly life without anger or fear to feed you."

"You know I don't understand Injun talk."

Carefully Loma formed the English words. "Big Jim need meat."

"You mean you're going out to kill a deer?"

Loma nodded.

"Well I'll be," Big Jim muttered. "I must be dead already and don't know it. Sure enough I'm hearing the voices of angels coming from the heavens."

Loma and Big Jim watched the winter go by. They saw the sun a little higher in the sky each day. And in front of the cabin where the snow was tracked down, little rivulets of water trickled off the path into the soft snow at the sides.

With his bow and arrows Loma kept them in meat for over a month and from the deer hide, Big Jim made them each a new pair of moccasins.

Big Jim's ribs were finally healing. Through his instructions, Loma cut tree limbs and watched while the trapper made a crude pair of crutches that enabled him to hobble around the cabin.

There came a morning that was sunny and warm; there was steam rising from the roof and the sound of snow melting everywhere, from the drip at the roof to the rush of the stream. Big Jim opened the cabin door and was surprised to find that it was warmer outside than it was in the cabin. He eased his back against the cabin wall and thought about Josie. In a couple of weeks he would be able to travel. There wasn't any use in staying here. The beaver pelts would be bad, as they always were when spring set in. What worried him most was that he didn't have enough pelts to make Josie rich as he had promised. Maybe they'd have to wait a spell longer before they got married. He shook the thought from his mind and listened to the smack of the horse's hoofs as Loma rode through the snow.

Loma called to him. "Big Jim! Big Jim!"

Big Jim scrambled up on his crutches, hobbled forward a few feet in the snow and stood half-blind in the sunlight, wondering what could have happened.

"Listen," Loma rode the horse up close to him.

Big Jim held his breath. There was urgency in the boy's voice.

"A man called. I heard him."

Big Jim didn't believe it. The same thing had happened to him before when he was alone in the mountains. Oftentimes he heard things and never found out what they were. He said nothing and listened. . . .

"Hey, anybody home?" They heard it together.

For a minute Big Jim stood perfectly still. Then he grinned. "That's Beaver Charlie!" He raised his head toward the sound and called back. Then he turned to Loma. "Go on down and meet him for me."

Loma was frightened. He didn't know why. Now that he knew it was a friend of Big Jim he ought to be glad. He had wished often enough that Big Jim had somebody to talk to other than himself. But now that someone was here, he was afraid.

"Go on. Do as I say. Charlie won't bite; he likes In-juns."

Loma suddenly realized that the only white man he knew was Big Jim. The idea of meeting a stranger startled him.

"Hurry, boy. Don't keep our guest waiting. It ain't polite."

From the slight shift of Loma's weight, the horse turned and moved south along the slushy snow trail. Behind a rise that blocked the cabin from view the boy met Beaver Charlie coming toward him on the same trail, riding a brown and white horse. In one quick glance Loma took in the strangely shaped beaver hat, the long gray beard that partially hid a jolly face, the short, stocky frame that had seen many years of work. For some reason the boy liked him immediately.

"Well, well," the jovial voice said. "You must be the Loma that Josie's been telling me so much about." He rode close and stuck out his weather-beaten hand.

Loma looked at the hand. He did not know what to do.

Beaver Charlie laughed. "This here's a white man's way of saying howdy. When we're glad to see somebody, we shake hands."

Loma smiled shyly as he extended his hand. "Hello, Beaver Charlie," he said.

"So you know me, do you? Some reputation I got. Where's that no-good trapper friend of mine?"

"He is waiting at cabin," Loma explained in careful English.

"Hey, you speak like an old-timer. How's Jim doing with Hopi talk?"

"Not well," Loma caught the gay mood of the old trapper.

Beaver Charlie roared with laughter. As they rode up the trail to the shed, he said, "I've seen good riders use no saddle, but I've never seen a horse rode without a bridle, too. You're pretty good."

Loma looked down at the horse's withers embarrassed— and proud.

94

Beaver Charlie inspected the feed room. "Didn't think this hay would last your horses through the winter. Looks like it's going to, though. Be able to turn 'em out on the mountain grass in a couple of weeks if the weather don't change for the worse." He walked around the shed slapping the horses on the rumps. "Good shape. Looks to me like an Indian boy I know spends most of his time brushing horses instead of trapping beaver."

Loma looked away, his eyes hooded from the old trapper.

"Hey, Loma. None of that. Lot of my best friends are Indians who feel the same way you do. I could've told Big Jim from the start what he was getting in for, but he's so darn stubborn I thought I'd let him find out for himself. Besides, I've a feeling you're about as stubborn as he is. Maybe you've taught him a thing or two." He put the weather-beaten hand under Loma's chin and turned his face toward him. "No hard feelings?" The blue eyes twinkled in good humor.

"You are fast with the words," Loma said smiling.

"Yep. They've gotten me out of many a jam. I'd have been shot more than once if I hadn't been smiling when I cussed some men out. But what am I doing telling you my trade secrets? Come on, let's go see that ugly grizzly who calls himself a man."

As they walked up the path leading from the shed to the cabin, Beaver Charlie cocked his strange hat comically to one side. "By the way, Loma, where's Big Jim keeping the beaver pelts?"

"In the feed room."

"In the feed room! Stop pulling my leg. There weren't more than a couple dozen pelts in there. Just saw 'em with my own eyes."

"I do not pull leg."

"Gallopin' goose eggs!" Beaver Charlie exclaimed at the stooped figure in the doorway. "Whatever you tangled with was a whole lot bigger than you!"

"Charlie! You stiff-jointed old . . . " The roar of Big Jim's voice cut off abruptly. He staggered, reeled around and caught hold of the cabin wall.

Loma ran to him, stood next to the big man until the color returned to his face, then helped him across the cabin floor in front of the fire. Slowly, painfully, Big Jim sat down.

Beaver Charlie stood mute.

Finally Big Jim's breath came back to him. "I guess these here busted ribs ain't up to shouting yet. Glad to see you, Charlie."

"Me too, only I hope that sort of thing don't happen too often. You nearly scared me out of my moccasins."

Big Jim grinned. "It's not every day we get visitors. What brings you into the mountains? You got the beaver fever?"

"No sir! I'm too old for that. Trapped my last beaver and glad of it, too. What I came for can wait. How long you been laid up?"

Big Jim looked at Loma. "What was the last count, five weeks?"

Loma nodded.

"Five weeks!"

"Almost six."

"Then Loma *was* telling the facts."

"'Bout what?" questioned the big man.

"About them pelts in the feed room being all you have."

"He was telling the facts," Big Jim agreed.

"Well thanks, Loma," Beaver Charlie said accepting a cup of coffee. "That's right thoughtful of you. You know, Jim, in one way you ought to be glad."

"About what?"

"Being laid up gives a man time to think about what he's been doing with himself and what he's going to do with himself. Trappers make quick money, but we spend it just as quick. How many years you been trapping?"

"Ten I'd say, give or take a year. What are you getting at?"

Beaver Charlie peered over the rim of his coffee cup. "Just this. I started trapping beaver in the east when I was a kid of fifteen. Now I'm better than sixty. Figures out to forty-five years or more. I've been rich a dozen times over and I've been flat busted more times than I've been rich. So where'd it get me?"

"What's all that got to do with me?"

"Everything. You've been trapping ten years. How much money you got saved?"

Big Jim frowned.

"Just as I thought. Comes quick, goes quick. It's a bad life. In the first place the beavers will soon be gone from here like they are in the east. Trappers stripped the rivers and streams of them. Ain't right. Beavers do a lot of good. Same thing's happening here, or will pretty soon, the way the trappers are coming into Santa Fe with their pelts. Won't be too many more years and there won't be a beaver left in the territory."

Big Jim shook his head. "You don't sound like yourself, Charlie. Who you been talking to?"

"Josie," Charlie blurted before thinking. Quickly he added, "She's right, too. Marry her, Jim. Settle down someplace. Wish I'd done it years ago. A man sure gets lonely."

"Look, Charlie, not that it's any of your business, but I don't plan to marry Josie until I can give her a decent life."

"Sure, that's what I said," Beaver Charlie held up his coffee cup for a refill. "Thanks, Loma. Come over here and sit yourself down next to me, boy. There, that's better. I like having kids around, never had none of my own. It's a sorry state of affairs when a man don't have any kids." He turned back to Big Jim. "I had me a wife all picked out once. Pretty she was, and a hard worker. I felt the same way you do about waiting to marry until I could give her the world in a sack of gold. Three years she waited—kept telling me the money wasn't important. I should've believed her, but no, I kept trapping beaver and blowing money, gambling and drinking. Know what finally happened? She ran off with a dirt farmer who didn't have nothing. He swung an ax instead of trapping and pretty soon he had a fine little farm. I saw her a couple years later, Jim . . . She had a little girl, prettiest thing you ever saw . . . and she was happy."

Big Jim held the coffee mug in both hands. He stared at the steam as it rose into his face. "It's not the same with Josie," he said softly. "She promised to wait."

"Sure, she's been promising for two years and she's held good to that promise, too. But she's lonely, Jim. There are lots of men in Santa Fe who have their eyes on Josie."

Sudden anger showed on Big Jim's face. He banged the coffee cup down. "What are you talking about!"

"Sure there are. What'd you expect? Josie's a good looker and she's as fine a woman as you'd hope to meet. Don't worry your stubborn head, she's gone out with no one. But I'm telling you it ain't fair to make a young woman like that stay home alone and wait and wait and wait until you come around. No sir, it ain't fair at all.''

The lines on Big Jim's forehead wrinkled into a frown. "Charlie, you saw for yourself how many beaver pelts I've got. 'Course I would have had more if the boy . . .''

"Now, Jim. It ain't right to blame the boy just because trapping don't appeal to him.''

Big Jim lifted his eyes to Loma who sat looking at the floor. "You're right, Charlie. About the boy anyhow; he saved my life . . . he and that old Injun.''

Beaver Charlie was surprised at the look in the trapper's eyes as he gazed at the boy.

Big Jim went on. "No, Loma's all right. He's done a man's work around here and sometimes what he says about killing actually makes a little bit of sense. For him of course. Not for me.''

Beaver Charlie glanced from Big Jim to Loma and back to Big Jim. Something had happened to the man; something Beaver Charlie couldn't put his finger on. Big Jim had always been a strange, somewhat ruthless breed of man who'd do most anything to get what he wanted. Now, as he looked at the trapper, he saw a new calm in his eyes. It was almost a peaceful look.

"Jim,'' drawled the old trapper. "Just how close to death were you?''

"Well, from the way I see it, death was knocking and the door was about half-open. That Injun friend of yours, Tall Walking Rain, and the boy found me half-frozen and pretty busted up. I was afraid I'd lose some of my face, but I sure didn't.''

"Tall Walking Rain, huh? Let me see that leg of yours.''

"What for? It'll be healed in another couple of weeks."

Beaver Charlie leaned forward while Loma removed the bandage from the opening in the splint. The bones were set straight with only a slight bulge at the shin. Sharp jagged lines showed where the bone had torn through the flesh. Although the skin flaps were bluish-purple, they had healed together perfectly. Only the slightest puffiness remained.

"Whew!" Beaver Charlie said sitting back on his haunches. "I ain't never seen one to top that. Looks to me if Tall Walking Rain hadn't been here, you'd be without a leg."

Big Jim grinned. "Wouldn't be surprised but what you're right."

Loma looked up from his cross-legged position beside Beaver Charlie. "Tall Walking Rain has much wisdom like Beaver Charlie."

Surprise crossed the old trapper's face. "Well, thanks, Loma. That's the finest compliment I ever had. But I ain't near so wise as the old Indian."

"The old Injun has an acid tongue if ever I heard one," Big Jim broke in. "But he can fix up busted legs, I'll give him that."

"His tongue ain't so acid unless he's got a deserving party," Beaver Charlie said with a wink. "I must admit he's used it on me some in the past too. Maybe that's one of the reasons he's the best friend I got. Never speaks nothing but the truth."

"Is Tall Walking Rain a medicine man?" Loma asked.

"You bet your life he is. In fact he's the best medicine man in the territory. Indians from Santa Fe and Rio Grande are always asking for his help when something really serious comes along. He never refuses either, walks through these mountains a couple times a year just to help the sick when he's needed. Don't know how he does it, most men his age have been under ground for twenty years. I'll tell you something else about him. When Tall Walking Rain says something, a person just naturally sits up and takes notice. Might make 'em mad as the devil, but that's cause the truth hurts and he don't spare the knockout punch where truth's needed. Then too, I've been with him for days at a time when he's not so much as spoken a word. Don't seem to matter either way somehow. A man feels better just being around him.''

"Big Jim gave Tall Walking Rain a horse to ride home."

Charlie thought he detected a hint of pride in the boy's voice. "That was mighty nice of you, Jim."

Big Jim grinned good-naturedly. "Sure was, after all the lecturing he gave me."

"I can see it now," Beaver Charlie laughed. "The old Indian sitting there talking about what's right and what's wrong, you wanting to get up and knock the stuffings out of him and not being able to move off the floor." He removed the tilted fur hat and slapped it against his leg. "Yessir, I'd have given my last nine teeth to see that."

Loma hid his smile by looking down at the floor.

Big Jim grinned. "I admit I found it kind of hard to believe myself. Charlie, you still haven't told us why you're here. Or did you just get plain lonesome for a couple of handsome faces?"

The laugh faded from Beaver Charlie's face. "The reason I'm here, Jim, has to do with Loma."

Both Big Jim and the boy looked up, surprised.

"I have a Hopi friend in Rio Grande name of Paati." He turned to Loma. "I doubt if you know him. He moved from the mesas before you were born. Anyhow, he told me a Hopi man name of Wickvaya traveled by himself all the way from Oraibi to the Rio Grande Valley. . . ."

I know Wickvaya," Loma whispered. "Oraibi is my village."

Beaver Charlie patted the boy's arm and went on. "Paati told me that Wickvaya plans to do everything he can about getting his wife and the Hopi children back to their rightful homes."

"This is Loma's rightful home!" Big Jim blurted. "There's nothing Wickvaya can do."

"Maybe. Maybe not. The chief of the Rio Grande Indians called in a man who could read and write, had him listen to Wickvaya's story and write down everything he heard."

"What for?" Anger was rising in Big Jim.

Beaver Charlie shrugged his shoulders. "For the record I guess."

"Since when did the Injuns start keeping written records?" Big Jim asked.

"Wasn't written for the Indians, Jim."

"Who, then?"

"The governor."

"The governor!" Big Jim almost shouted.

"Paati said that Wickvaya and three men left Rio Grande headed for Santa Fe to see the governor."

Loma felt his heart pound wildly beneath the buckskin shirt. Wickvaya was a brave Hopi. In spite of the raiders and the bad snowstorms, he had made it across the desert alone. He must concentrate on sending good thoughts in Wickvaya's direction.

"You don't think the governor will see them, do you?" Big Jim asked in a strange voice.

"Don't know. Hopis are a stubborn people, as you've no doubt found out." He winked at Loma. "They won't cause any trouble, but they'll be persistent, you can count on that."

"We paid for the kids. Legally they're ours."

Beaver Charlie shook his head. "I don't know, Jim. Rumor had it that the slaves who were sold that day were Navajos. The governor didn't care much, because the Navajos are always raiding Santa Fe and stealing horses from the Spaniards. When he hears the kids were Hopi, he might see things a little different."

"They aren't going to get Loma! I'll hide him up here until it blows over."

Beaver Charlie got up, went to the fire and poured himself another cup of coffee. "Won't work," he said calmly.

"Why not? Who'd know?"

Beaver Charlie looked directly into Big Jim's fearful eyes. "I would," he said.

For two weeks Beaver Charlie stayed with he mountain man and the Indian boy, waiting for Big Jim's ribs to heal enough so he could travel. That they were well into the month of April could be told by the new height of the sun, by the feel of the air, by the furry green buds on the branches and twigs high overhead. It was the start of spring. Soon the birds would be back and the sleepy animals would come out of their winter homes.

Loma went out of the cabin to the shed. He fed the horses and while they were eating, he walked out into the forest alone. He walked through the pines and aspen trees toward the stream. He missed being able to see the vast desert that stretched in every direction. In his village the children would soon be going barefoot. They would not have moccasins on their feet again until the air turned cold in the fall. And the men would soon be working the small fields, planting corn beneath the blue skies.

In the spring the clans would go for young eagles, bring them back to the villages and raise them for the Niman

Kachina ceremony later on in the summer. It was the time of year when Hopi men, women and children sang songs from morning until night. It was the time of games and spring dances. It was the time of laughter and running. There would be none of this for Loma, at least not this year. Perhaps if Wickvaya convinced someone that the Hopi children should be returned . . . perhaps then he would see his family again. In the meantime he must wait and in the waiting he must try to ease the longing in his heart.

He followed along a deerpath, going slowly, hoping to catch a glimpse of a doe or a buck. As he neared the stream there was a glint of sun on it and steam rising from its wet banks. He stepped out on a rock and felt the warmth of it rise up to meet him. He squatted down closer to the rock and noticed little shoots of grass pushing their way out of the melting ice at the water's edge.

After awhile he stood up, hopped from the rock and went back toward the cabin. When he neared the door he heard Beaver Charlie and Big Jim arguing.

"The boy and I are staying here, Charlie. Go on ahead if you want."

"I aim to," Charlie said flatly. "But you're coming with me, both of you."

"That's a mighty strong order."

"I'm a mighty strong man. Now listen, Jim. Spring is almost here. The beaver will be moulting. You know as well as I do that their fur is no good in the spring."

"I ain't thinking of beaver!" Big Jim roared.

"You ain't thinking at all! We got no idea if Wickvaya talked to the governor and even if he did, we don't know that the governor will do anything about the kids."

"I ain't taking the chance."

"Jim, Loma has a family. Just because you paid money for him don't mean he belongs to you. What's the matter with you, anyhow? Never seen you act this way before. Buy yourself another slave, one who'll be willing to help trap beaver for you."

"Thought you said trapping beaver was a bad life."

"I did."

"Well, maybe, just maybe, I think so too."

"Good. Marry Josie then."

"I aim to!"

"Then there's no need for talk. Your ribs are healed enough for travel. Let's start packing."

"I told you I ain't leaving until this thing blows over."

Beaver Charlie let out an exasperated breath. "Now you listen to me. If the governor sends out orders to gather up all the captured kids, they'll be coming up here in the mountains to get Loma. If he don't issue the orders, then Loma's just as safe with you in Santa Fe. It don't matter where you are; if they want him, they'll find him. Can you get that through your thick head?"

"I paid good money for the boy. He's my slave and they ain't going to. . . ."

"If it's the money you're worried about, I'll buy him from you myself. Then you ornery critter . . . you can stay up here in the mountains until Hades freezes over."

"It's not the money!" Big Jim thundered. "He ain't for sale!"

Beaver Charlie looked up at the big man quizzically. "Jim," he said, "I believe you've gone soft on the boy."

"You're crazy!" Big Jim shouted.

Beaver Charlie nodded knowingly. "Okay, then let me ask you . . . have you thought about what Loma wants?"

An anxious expression crossed Big Jim's eyes. "Why should I? He's been happy enough here with me. Bet he's forgotten all about his family. He hasn't mentioned them, not once."

"Then we'll leave it up to him," Charlie suggested.

"The devil we will. I give the orders around here!"

"In that case you won't mind if I ask him, just for curiosity."

The fire left Big Jim's eyes. "No," he said slowly. "Don't say anything to the boy, Charlie. I don't want him to think . . . Never mind. When he comes in, I'll tell him myself."

Loma sat down outside the cabin with the sun in his face, but not in his eyes. His mind raced, but he didn't want to think, so he lifted his thoughts up toward the sun and waited. After awhile he rose, brushed the wet snow from his buckskin pants and walked slowly inside.

Big Jim turned his head carefully. "I never knew it to take anyone so long to feed the horses as it does you, especially when there's more important work to be done."

Loma's eyes questioned him.

Beaver Charlie looked up from the buffalo robe he was folding. "Springtime's almost here. It's time we left for Santa Fe. Now how about giving us a hand with the packing?"

Loma nodded. He dared not speak for fear the words would betray the joy in his heart.

There was so little food left that it was packed in one large bag. Loma dragged the bag over near the door. He stuffed his new moccasins in a small leather pouch, took the bow and arrows from the wall and happily tossed them in the fire.

"Hey," Big Jim complained. "We might need those."

Loma ignored this. In Santa Fe there would be no need for him to hunt meat, especially if the governor . . . No, he must not think of that yet.

In less than thirty minutes they were packed, the fire had been put out and the cabin cleaned as well as they thought necessary. Beaver Charlie bolted the cabin door after Big Jim and Loma carried the food, clothing, and trapping equipment to the shed. Charlie picked up what was left behind and followed. Soon the horses were saddled and packed.

As they rode away from the shed Big Jim said, "This summer I'll bring a buckboard load of hay up here for you, Charlie. Afraid my horses nearly cleaned you out."

"You can buy me a buckboard load of hay," Charlie agreed, "but there's no need to bring it all the way up here. That is, unless you plan on coming back next winter."

Big Jim didn't answer.

"Feel the air," Beaver Charlie said, stretching both arms straight out. "It's spring sure enough."

Loma smiled. "How does the air feel?"

"Soft, full of fine smells. Winter air is empty and crisp. But come spring and the air is filled with all sorts of new life. After the snow melts the grass pops up so quick you can almost hear it growing."

"Look up there," Big Jim said getting the feel of spring himself, "at the little leaves perched up on the highest branches. In a couple of weeks they'll be big enough to put shade on the ground."

"Yep," agreed Charlie. "But before that happens, there'll be wild flowers sprouting up through the snow, drinking in the sun as fast as they can before the leaves shut out the sun from them."

108

"Soon the birds will fly," Loma said.

"Won't be long at that," Charlie agreed. "'Course birds ain't good for much, too small for eating and most of 'em are nothing but bones. But there's something about birds that makes 'em nice to have around."

On and on they rode, working steadily through the mountains, riding in and out through the tall spruce and pine and aspen trees. The stream off to the right was some distance away, but close enough for them to hear the rushing water. There was a small breeze from the south that brought a little chill to the sun-warmed air.

The horses felt good, too. They walked, ears pricked forward, through the wet snow. Oftentimes they snorted at nothing in particular, more as a release of all the energy pent up during the long winter months. Some of their long hair had begun to shed off in big splotches along their necks, showing sleek spring coats of short hair beneath.

Beaver Charlie whistled a tune unfamiliar to Loma, but well-known to Big Jim, who joined in.

Loma turned his thoughts inward and his mind stirred the memory of his village high on the mesas, of his mother and father, of his friends and his people. Only in his memory could he be with them now, and he realized that only in his memory did the cabin, the injured beaver, and the trip to find Big Jim keep on living. Only in his memory could he recall Tall Walking Rain and his words of wisdom. The things that were happening now would be memories tomorrow. His father had said that memory is like the stream which flows beneath the ground. "It is the wise man," he had said, "who fills his stream with pure water."

As evening shadows stretched out across the mountains Beaver Charlie stopped his horse. "This is a likely looking spot to hole up for the night. What do you say?"

Big Jim slipped off the saddle and leaned heavily against the horse. "None too soon to suit me," he admitted.

"How are them ribs of yours making out?"

"Being busted up saps a man's strength some, I'll say that. I'm okay though, or at least will be after a hot cup of coffee and some jerky."

"I will take care of the horses," Loma offered.

Big Jim nodded, found a bare patch of ground under a big pine tree and sat down. Slowly he eased his back against the trunk. "There now," he told himself, "you'll be just fine."

Loma unsaddled and unbridled the horses, tied a rawhide thong on their hind legs and let them go. Beaver Charlie grinned. "Loma, you've got the hobbles on the wrong legs. They go in front."

"It is so they . . ." He tried to think of the correct English. "It is so they step in snow for grass."

"You mean *paw* through the snow," Big Jim called from the tree.

Loma nodded. "Yes, paw is the word. Tall Walking Rain show me."

"Humph. Never heard of putting hobbles on the hind legs. Hope the horses ain't twenty miles off in the mountains by morning." Charlie started to tie the rawhide thong on the hind legs of his horse, then changed his mind. "Nope, ain't going to take the chance. I'm too old to go hiking all over the mountains trying to catch up to my horse."

"They will stay," Loma insisted.

"Maybe, but I ain't going to chance it just the same."

"Your horse walk many miles today. How will he eat?"

"The snow's soft. He can shove his head through it for what grass he needs."

Loma didn't argue.

"All right, Jim. What'll you have—a white man's fire or an Indian fire?"

"A white man's fire. I don't want to freeze to death."

Loma looked at them, puzzled.

Almost in earnest, Beaver Charlie explained. "Indians make little bitty fires, squat around them to keep warm. White men always build big fires, stand half a mile away so they won't get burned."

Loma thought about it and decided it was true.

Before the coffee pot was empty, Big Jim's head nodded forward and he was asleep. Suddenly his eyes flew open and he looked around sheepishly. When he saw that Beaver Charlie and the boy were not paying any attention, he set the coffee cup down and curled up on the buffalo robe. In a few minutes he was snoring.

Loma covered the big trapper with the edge of the buffalo robe and went back to the fire. Beaver Charlie yawned. "Riding all day's hard work for an old codger. Guess I'll turn in."

Loma sat huddled under the bearskin looking at the stars. The words of Tall Walking Rain came to him as he stared into the sky. *Truth is a bright star dropped from the heart of eternity.* He wasn't sure he understood that at all.

The next morning the two saddle horses and the two pack horses Loma had hobbled were close to camp. Beaver Charlie's horse was nowhere to be seen. The old trapper scowled beneath the beaver-fur hat, mumbled something under his breath and went out looking for his horse.

By the time he returned to camp, Loma and Big Jim had saddled and packed the four horses and were waiting.

"If either one of you so much as says, 'I told you so,' I'll. . ."

Big Jim roared with laughter. Loma turned his eyes toward the ground.

When Beaver Charlie was saddled, they all mounted and turned the horses south toward Santa Fe. All morning Charlie and Big Jim sang trapper songs, leaving out the swear words for Loma's sake.

It was early afternoon when Beaver Charlie reined his horse in abruptly. "Hey, Loma, Jim. Look!" he exclaimed softly. "Over to our left."

There, in an opening, standing in the full sunlight was a black mother bear and her two cubs. The nearsighted mother bear had heard the horses, but she couldn't make out the riders. She rose on her hind legs for a better look, then suddenly raised her paw, spanked both of her cubs and sent them scurrying up a nearby sapling.

Big Jim grinned. "Ever watch bears much, boy?"

Loma shook his head. "I see only one bear before, on journey to salt caves."

"Well, they're something to watch all right. Those baby cubs will stay up that little tree until she tells them it's safe to come down. That's the first lesson they learn when they come out of their cave in the spring."

"Yeah," Beaver Charlie agreed. "From now on whenever anything scary happens, the babies will scoot up a sapling. Nothing dumb about bears."

They kicked the horses forward down the trail away from the mother bear and her cubs. The mother bear stood blinking her eyes in the bright sunlight watching them go.

"She is not afraid," Loma said.

"Sure she is," Beaver Charlie threw in. "Black bear are mighty timid, but they're too doggone lazy to run. The grizzly ain't lazy, no sir. There's nothing lazy about them, but these black bear are nothing like the grizzly. The black bear love deer meat, but they're too lazy to chase one down. Same with the ground squirrels and gophers. Black bear love the taste of them, but the work it takes to dig them out of their dens don't appeal to 'em. A grizzly though, would uproot a whole hillside to get a half-dozen gophers. Don't know what makes 'em so different from each other, but they sure are."

"What do the black bear eat?" asked Loma.

Big Jim answered. "Wild honey, if they can get it. Or the big brown mushrooms. And they like puffballs. In the summer black bear live mostly on berries. Sometimes they'll eat the larvae out of . . ." Pain crossed his face. He dropped the reins, leaned over the pummel and took his leg out of the stirrup.

"What's the matter?" Charlie rode up beside him.

"Nothing. This leg is screaming at me, that's all."

"Want to stop awhile?"

"Nope. It's fine now."

"You've been laid up a long time, Jim. If this riding's too much for you, shout out."

Big Jim forced a grin. "The day I can't keep up with a broken-down old trapper like you will be a cold day in August."

"Oh, yeah. When the time comes you think you can out-ride me . . ."

Loma relaxed in the saddle. Big Jim would be all right.

After four days and three nights the two men and the boy arrived in Santa Fe. It was dusk and the riders were tired. Big Jim reined his horse down a side street toward the town stable. Loma followed.

"Hey, wait!" Beaver Charlie called after them.

Big Jim turned in the saddle. "What for? I want to get the horses taken care of, then head over to Josie's."

"Cost money to stable the horses in town," Charlie said. "Bring 'em on over to my place. I've enough oats for tonight and tomorrow morning, besides a good-sized pasture."

"Charlie, I've used your cabin all winter. That's enough."

"Hate to see a good cabin go to waste, better that it's lived in. You're going to pay me back for the hay and oats. Far as the pasture's concerned, my old horse has been alone so much that he'll enjoy the company. And more important, if your horses are at my place I can make darn sure that you haven't taken Loma and run off somewhere."

Big Jim grinned. "Trusting old coot, aren't you?"

They turned left down another side street and followed it out to the edge of town. Soon they arrived in front of a small stone house surrounded by grass pasture. After unsaddling and unpacking the horses, Charlie brought out the oats, fed each horse, then Loma turned them into the pasture. Usually the horses would have bucked and kicked, glad to be out of the snow and in the green grass, but tonight they were too tired. Instead of running around, they lowered their heads to the grass and ate.

"Know just how they feel," sympathized Big Jim. "I'm half-starved myself. Charlie, come on over to Josie's with the boy and me. We'll get ourselves a home-cooked meal."

"Maybe tomorrow. Tonight you and Josie will want to be alone. Why don't you leave Loma with me?"

A shine came into Big Jim's eyes, then he shook his head. "Nope. Won't hear of it. Josie will want to see both of you. We've got a whole lifetime to be alone when we choose to. Josie would want it this way even if I don't."

"Okay," Charlie agreed. "But the least we can do is go inside and get cleaned up. Wouldn't do for the likes of us to smell up her house."

An hour later they walked across the flats to the path that curved and circled among the rocks to Josie's house. Through the window Loma saw her sitting in the dim light reading. Big Jim knocked.

The door opened slowly, just a crack. Suddenly the door was all the way open and Big Jim was holding Josie in his strong arms. Loma and Beaver Charlie moved away from the light in the doorway into the night shadows. Charlie took a large red handkerchief from his back pocket and blew his nose. Loma watched Big Jim and Josie out of the corner of his eye. He didn't want to, but he couldn't help it.

Josie said, "Charlie has been away for over three weeks. I thought something had happened to you."

Big Jim laughed. "In a way it did. Let's go inside and we'll tell you about it."

Loma and Charlie came out of the shadows. Josie smiled happily. She took Loma's hands. "You look fine," she said. "Come in, Charlie, and tell me what happened."

While Josie fixed dinner the three of them sat around the table. Big Jim and Charlie drank coffee and told her about the accident. Her eyes turned to Loma. "You are very brave," she said.

Loma looked away.

"Brave! What do you mean, brave?" roared Big Jim. "I'm the one who was hurt."

Josie smiled. "He was very brave to stay with you when he had a chance to leave."

"Humph," Big Jim grunted.

Food had never tasted so good to Loma and he thought by the silence at the table that Big Jim and Charlie must feel the same. Josie was too excited to eat. She picked at the food, finally laid her fork aside and gazed happily at Big Jim.

After the dinner Charlie picked up the conversation. He knew Big Jim did not want to talk about it, but they would have to find out sooner or later.

"Heard anything more about Wickvaya?" he asked.

Big Jim scowled. "We got better things to talk about."

Loma held his breath.

"Yes," said Josie. "Wickvaya and his friends arrived in Santa Fe the same day you left, Charlie. They asked to see the Spanish captain in the governor's palace, but the guards would not let them in because the captain was sick. Wickvaya and the men waited a long time. Finally, they asked the guard to take the captain the written paper which had the story of the raid in Oraibi on it.''

"The guard didn't do it, did he?" Big Jim asked hopefully.

"Why, yes," said Josie. "He did."

"What'd the captain say?" Big Jim demanded.

Josie continued, "Wickvaya and the men waited outside the palace to see what would happen. In a short time the guard came back and said that the captain would see them."

"I thought he was sick," Big Jim murmured to himself.

Josie looked at him. "He was, but he saw Wickvaya and the three men from Rio Grande anyway. They went inside to find the captain sitting up in bed reading the written paper they had sent. When he finished reading the paper he was so angry that he jumped out of bed."

Anxiously, Big Jim asked. "And he tore the paper up?"

"No," Josie said. "The captain had Wickvaya repeat the story through an interpreter. When Wickvaya finished, the captain wrote a note to the governor personally."

Big Jim sank back in the chair. "I suppose," he said sarcastically, "that the governor welcomed them with open arms."

"Yes, he did," Josie said, confused by Big Jim's attitude. "He read the letter, then as the captain had done, the governor had Wickvaya repeat the story through an interpreter. The governor said he did not know that any such expedition had gone out until long after they had come back to Santa Fe. The report given him was that the children the soldiers brought back were Navajo."

Big Jim groaned.

"Are you all right?" she asked, concerned.

"Yeah, go on."

"Well, for that reason he did not pay much attention to the matter. . . ."

"For what reason?" Big Jim asked encouraged.

"For the reason the governor thought the children were Navajo."

"Oh," he moaned.

She glanced at him, puzzled. Charlie nodded. "Don't pay him no never mind. Go on with the news."

Josie hesitated, then continued. "The Navajo are not well-liked by the Spanish, because the Navajo steal their horses."

"Don't blame the Navajo a bit," growled Big Jim.

Josie ignored the comment. "The governor assured Wickvaya that he would get his wife and the Hopi children back to Santa Fe as soon as possible so Wickvaya could take them home to their mothers and fathers."

Big Jim sat forward. "By the time the Spaniards make up their minds to do anything about it, we'll be long gone from here. They're slower in making decisions than one of those black bears we saw the other day."

Josie shook her head. "Not this time, Jim. The next day the governor called fifty guardsmen and instructed them to bring in every man who had been on the raiding expedition, plus all the Hopi children who had been sold."

"How long ago was that?"

"About a week. Perhaps more. I think we should tell Loma."

Big Jim sat in mute silence.

Beaver Charlie grinned. "Don't have to tell him nothing, Josie. Loma's pretty good at understanding English."

A pleased expression crossed Josie's face. "Is that true, Loma?"

118

The boy nodded. "This gobner," he began.

"Governor," Big Jim growled.

"Yes," said Loma and went on, "Spaniards do what he say?"

Josie smiled. "The governor," she explained, "is the chief of Santa Fe and all the New Mexico territory around Santa Fe."

Loma's excitement grew. If the governor was the chief, then his word was the final word. He and the other children would be returned to Oraibi. If it did not take too long he would be there in time for Niman Kachina and the Snake-Antelope ceremonies. Then he looked at Big Jim. It would not be easy to leave him.

"I wonder," Charlie broke the silence, "what the governor wants with the men who raided the Hopi village?"

"Probably wants to raise their salary," said Big Jim moodily.

"It has been rumored," said Josie softly, "that he wishes to punish them."

Charlie nodded. "Hope so. Sure would put an end to stealing Indian kids, no matter what kind they were. I don't hold with selling child slaves. Don't hold with no kind of slavery."

"Charlie, sometimes you don't make any sense at all."

"Maybe, but I had my taste of it and I'm truthful in saying it didn't settle too well."

Big Jim sat up, interested. "Charlie, you old codger, you never told me you owned slaves."

"Who said anything about owning 'em? My ma and pa were poor. They needed money."

Big Jim's eyes grew wide. "You mean your ma and pa sold you just as if you were an Injun?"

"What's being Indian got to do with it? Kids have been

sold for a long time, Jim. Don't matter what breed they are.''

"Well, I'll be darned. How'd you get free?''

"Oh, my folks only bonded me out for two years, but that was enough to set a bad taste in my mouth.''

Big Jim had nothing to say. The four of them sat in silence. Finally Josie asked, "Charlie, how long will you stay in Santa Fe?''

Beaver Charlie shrugged his shoulders. "Don't know, Josie. Depends on a lot of things. But I ain't a man to stay put too long. Time I was moving on.''

"Moving on to where?'' shouted Big Jim. "What's the matter with Santa Fe?''

"Nothing. But I got me an itch. Seven years ago when I came to Santa Fe, I was just passing through. But I sort of liked it here, so I stayed. Now the itch needs scratching so I'm going to do what I came to do in the first place.''

"Charlie,'' Josie broke in. "Stop teasing and tell him.''

Charlie winked at Jim. "She's already telling a man what to do and she ain't even married yet. Better watch out, Jim, or you'll have a nagging woman on your hands.''

Josie and Big Jim smiled. "Best do as she says,'' Big Jim added, "if you know what's good for you.''

"Yes, ma'm,'' he said with a twinkle. "The last few years of trapping I saved me up some money. Not much mind you, but enough to start me a little Indian trading post.''

Big Jim squinted at the old man. "You feel all right?''

"Never felt better. I've had the idea tucked away inside my head ever since I left the east.''

"You're talking like a man who's been out in the sun too long.''

"Maybe. But the way I see it, the Indians are fine people. It ain't too often that a white man gives 'em a fair shake. I'd like to change that."

"You'll go broke before a year's up."

"I don't aim to get rich. Then again, I don't aim to go broke. There's a living to be made from trading posts, a good, decent living."

"Sure, if you don't mind starving for awhile. Where do you aim to do all this?"

"Arizona."

"Arizona!" he roared. "What's in Arizona but a bunch of thieving Navajos?"

"The Navajos ain't all thieves, you can't say that."

"Okay, but why Arizona?"

"Well, Arizona's got Apaches, Papagos, Pimas and Hopis. Apaches pretty much take care of themselves, don't know as it'd do to have a trading post near them. Then too, they get mighty cantankerous. Think what I'll probably do is buy from some of the towns up in the northern part of Arizona, then take a buckboard around to the Navajos and Hopis, trading what they need. After awhile, I'll be able to tell where a good place for a permanent trading post would be. But I've made up my mind on Arizona."

"You will come to Oraibi?" Loma asked hopefully.

Beaver Charlie shrugged his shoulders. "Can't rightly say, Loma. But it wouldn't surprise me none if I was to stop by there and say howdy."

"The Hopis haven't any gold. You'd be wasting your time."

"No, they ain't got gold, that's true, but Paati says they make fine pottery on First Mesa and he says there's not a basket in the world can compare to what the women make on Second and Third Mesas."

"You don't believe that stuff!"

Loma spoke out. "What he says is true."

Josie nodded in agreement.

"Look," Big Jim blurted. "You take a buckboard loaded with supplies out alone in that country and you'll be raided and scalped the first night."

"That's a chance I'm willing to take."

"Josie, say something. Tell him what a darn fool he is!"

Josie looked kindly at Big Jim. "I think it is a fine thing he is going to do. Charlie is a fair man. The Indians will know this and protect him."

"I will teach you to speak Hopi," Loma offered.

"Well now, thanks, Loma. I might just take you up on that. Be a handy thing to know."

"The first thing you'd better teach him is how to yell for help."

"Hopi are the people of peace," Loma explained.

"I'm thinking of the Navajo," Big Jim relented.

"Don't you worry none," Charlie insisted.

"Worry! What makes you think I'd waste my time worrying about an old coot like you? And, boy, what makes you say the Hopi are peaceful? Look what they're doing coming to the governor and stirring up trouble."

Josie moved closer to Jim and placed her hand lightly on his arm. "Wickvaya's wife was taken from him. If your wife were captured, would you not go after her?"

"Try and stop me!" he roared. Then, suddenly realizing what he had said, "But that's different."

"Why different?" she asked gently.

"Well, because . . ." he grinned sheepishly. "I ain't a man of peace."

Charlie stretched, got up from the chair and yawned. "I'm plumb worn out. So's Loma. We'll go on over to my house. Come on when you're ready, Jim."

"Okay, Charlie. Think I'll stay with Josie awhile longer. But I'll be coming soon. Those four days of riding did me in."

They thanked Josie for the dinner, Charlie set the fur hat at a tilt on his head and they started toward his house in the darkness.

As they walked along across the flats Loma questioned the old trapper. "If Big Jim is tired, why does he stay?"

"They got things to talk over that don't concern you and me."

Loma thought this over. Then he asked, "Do you think Santa Fe chief will send Hopi children home to Oraibi?"

"I ain't sure, Loma. But the way things look, you and the other kids will be heading for home before too much longer. Bet you'll be mighty glad to see your ma and pa."

Loma lifted his eyes to the stars. Beyond the earth, beyond the clouds, beyond the sky, beyond the moon, the breath of the wind had taken his prayers. Some months ago he thought that living without his people would be like living in an empty dwelling beside a dead fire. Tonight he was suddenly grateful for having been one of the captured children.

"You're a puzzle," Beaver Charlie said when Loma caught up to him. "Ain't you glad to be going home?"

"I am glad."

"You know, Loma," Charlie said picking up the boy's mood. "In a way you're lucky. The way the west's being overrun with white men, they'll soon be coming around the Hopi mesas. You have a head start in knowing how to deal with 'em.

"Yes. What I have learned will help my people."

"It ain't right to limit help to your people alone. You know, we whites ain't such a bad sort. Mostly overgrown kids with a burning desire for adventure."

Loma smiled. "Indian and the white man breathe the same air as the mountains."

"Yeah, I never thought of it that way. We're all made out of the same stuff all right. 'Course not everybody sees it that way. There're some men who think the only good Indian is a dead Indian. There're some who forget to listen to their hearts and they get carried away looking for gold, making money, stepping on anyone who gets in their way. They're the troublemakers. But they ain't the whole story."

As they entered the small stone house, Beaver Charlie pointed to a straw mat. Loma curled up on it and tucked the buffalo robe close around him. He lay for a long time wondering why he was not able to sleep. Finally he tiptoed out of the house leaving the snoring Charlie inside, wrapped the buffalo robe around him and lay on the ground. He looked up at the stars that dotted eternity. In a few moments he was asleep.

"Don't stand there knocking all day," Big Jim roared at the closed door. "Come on in."

The door to Charlie's stone house opened and a tall Spanish guardsman stood in the doorway.

Big Jim leaped to his feet. "What in the devil do you want?"

The Spanish guardsman stood at attention. "I have come for the Hopi boy."

"Charlie, you understand Spanish. What's this yahoo want?"

Beaver Charlie looked up under his bushy gray eyebrows. "He's asking for Loma."

Loma's eyes grew wide. Beneath the buckskin shirt his heart quickened.

"Okay!" boomed Big Jim. "You've asked. Now get out of here!"

"I have orders to seize the boy," the Spanish guardsman snapped.

Charlie placed a restraining hand on Big Jim's shoulder.

"Got a copy of them orders?" he asked the uniformed man.

The guardsman shoved a piece of rolled paper at Charlie. "Signed by the governor himself," he said in a sharp voice.

Charlie looked at Big Jim. "Signed by the governor."

"I don't care if it's signed by the king of . . ."

"Easy, Jim. These here orders are legal. If you don't let him take Loma, they'll come after him at gunpoint."

Big Jim grabbed the paper from Charlie. It was written in Spanish. He shoved it back to the guardsman. "Now you listen to me . . ."

Beaver Charlie interrupted. In Spanish he said, "We thought maybe the governor had changed his mind. It's been quite awhile since Wickvaya talked to him."

"His mind has not changed," the guardsman said. "One of the Hopi children by the name of Masavehma was taken to La Junta by his new family. It has taken us time to reach him. This boy is the last."

Hearing the familiar name Loma came forward. He looked up at Beaver Charlie. "He spoke of Masavehma?"

"Yeah. Said his new family had taken him to La Junta. I suppose he means Colorado."

"Masavehma is all right?" Loma inquired.

"Loma here is asking about Masavehma," Charlie said to the guardsman.

The guard stared straight ahead. "I have no time to waste. Tell the boy to come with me."

"Just a darn minute. Loma wants to know if his friend is okay. I intend that you give him an answer."

"Masavehma is well. The new family did not mistreat him. The boy will come with me now."

Charlie translated. "Your friend's okay. The guard

wants you to go with him, Loma. We'll drop by before you leave Santa Fe and see that everything's okay.''

Big Jim gritted his teeth. "Loma isn't going anywhere with this tin soldier. I'll take him to town myself.''

Charlie nodded. To the guard he said, "We'll bring the boy into town ourselves. He'll want to say goodbye to Josie and the horses before he leaves.''

Anger flared in the guardsman's voice. "No! He must come now!''

"What are you in such an all-fangled hurry about?'' Charlie asked.

"I have my orders. The Hopi children must be in town this afternoon to witness the punishment meted out to their captors.''

"What kind of punishment?''

"I do not know.''

"Knowing you Spaniards, I doubt whether Loma here would care to watch.''

The guardsman drew in a deep breath. His eyes narrowed. "I have no time to argue. The boy must come with me now!''

Charlie turned to Big Jim and Loma. "This here guardsman is pretty serious about the whole affair. The governor wants the Hopi kids to watch the punishment of the soldiers who captured them. I suppose it's so the kids will tell their people how the wicked soldiers were punished for mistaking the peaceful Hopis for raiding Navajos, or something like that.''

"It figures,'' Big Jim growled. "Tell him we'll bring Loma into town ourselves and tell him to get out of here. I'm tired of looking at his mean face.''

"Already made the suggestion," Charlie told Big Jim. "He says Loma has to go with him right now."

Big Jim's strong hands curled into fists. He raised one tight fist in front of the guardsman. The guardsman stepped back, surprised. "I told you we'd bring him in. I'm a lot of things, but I'm not a liar. Now move out of the doorway before I . . ."

The guardsman moved back, unholstered his gun and pointed it at Big Jim.

"Okay. Okay," Charlie spoke in rapid Spanish, "you've made your point. Give us a few minutes for goodbyes." Before the guardsman could answer, Charlie slammed the door.

"Jim," breathed Beaver Charlie, "don't do things like that. You're liable to get yourself killed."

"Well, who does he think he is, marching right up and demanding the boy? Knew I should have kept Loma in the mountains with me."

"Sooner or later they would have caught up with you. Shucks, they went clear to La Junta, Colorado, for . . . what's your friend's name?" he asked Loma.

"Masavehma."

"Yeah, that's it. If they went that far for him, they'd go into the mountains for Loma. You can't beat 'em, Jim. Loma has a right to be with his people."

Big Jim stood by the window. Suddenly his eyes lighted. "Hey, the tin soldier is riding away. Don't suppose he's changed his mind, do you?"

Charlie and Loma went to the window. Charlie shook his head. "Nope. It's my bet that he's going for reinforcements."

Big Jim nodded. "Wouldn't be surprised but what you're

right. Well, I took the boy from town in the first place and if anyone takes him back, it's going to be me. Think we have time to stop by Josie's on the way?''

"Sure we do," agreed Charlie. "Come on."

Halfway across the flats they saw Josie running to meet them. She was out of breath. "The guardsmen . . ." she panted, "they came to my house for Loma!"

"We know," Big Jim said, steadying her with his arm. "One of them just left Charlie's."

After catching her breath she slipped gently away from Big Jim and went to Loma. Her eyes looked into his. "Tomorrow they will take you back to your people," she said in Tewa.

Loma waited.

"Big Jim has grown fond of you. It is difficult for him to give you up. He thinks of you as his own son."

Loma wanted to say something, but the words caught in his throat.

"In two weeks," she went on, "Big Jim and I will be married by my people. Tomorrow we will be married the white man's way."

"You will marry two times?" Loma asked in a cracked voice.

"Yes. That is the way we want it." She looked deep into his dark eyes. "I have much to thank you for."

Loma looked away embarrassed. "No. Because of me Big Jim has no money for you. I could not trap the beaver."

She placed her hand gently under his chin and turned his face to meet her. "Because of you, Big Jim and I will marry soon. Because of you he wants sons of his own."

Tears glistened in Loma's eyes. "It does not matter about the money?"

She smiled. "Money cannot feed my spirit, Loma. Love is the food of the spirit. You have given the kind of love even a mountain man cannot fight. Last night Big Jim and I were sitting outside under the stars. He told me how the lifetime of a man is like the rising and setting sun. His words went like this, 'A good man will leave a good sunset. I don't aim to leave a stormy sky behind me, by golly. If it takes me the rest of my life doing things I've never done before, I'm going to leave a fine sunset. You can depend on that.'"

Loma's lower lip quivered. He forced a smile to steady it. He started to say something, then . . .

"Josie," Big Jim placed his hand on her shoulder. "I hate to butt in like this when you and the boy are talking, but if we are going to get Loma into town before the tin soldiers get back, we'd best be on our way."

Josie patted Loma's hands. He gazed into her steady blue eyes. Finally he turned and walked with the three of them toward town. Before they had gone very far, they heard the hum and shouting of a large crowd.

"Leaping river snakes!" shouted Charlie above the noise. "Everybody in Santa Fe must be here."

As they turned off the narrow back street onto the main street of town, it seemed horses and dogs and dust and people were everywhere. Big Jim stopped, stretched his neck to look over the crowd, then pointed toward the other end of the plaza.

"There's a bunch of kids being guarded by some soldiers over there." He lifted Loma into the air above his head. "Are they Hopi kids?"

Loma strained to see through the dust. His heart leaped. "Yes. They are Hopi."

Big Jim returned him to the ground. "They the stolen bunch?" he asked.

Loma nodded.

"All right. Josie, Charlie, follow us." Big Jim took Loma by the hand and led them through the crowd. It was the first time the man had ever held Loma's hand. The grip was sure and good. Loma felt the strength flow from Big Jim into his own body. He must not be afraid. But he was afraid! He couldn't help it.

After what seemed to Loma a long time, they arrived at the group of children from Oraibi. The children stood huddled together. Only their eyes expressed their uncertainty as to what was going to happen.

Big Jim squatted down beside him. "Well, boy, we're here. Before you get together with your friends, I got something I want to tell. . . . Hey, what's the big idea!" Big Jim shouted as a group of soldiers pushed him back into the crowd away from Loma.

Loma ran forward toward Big Jim, but a soldier caught him by the arm and dragged him toward a guardsman. "Here he is," the soldier said, holding the struggling boy.

The guardsman looked down from where he sat his horse. Loma recognized him as the same man who had been at Charlie's house earlier that day. The guardsman spurred the horse forward. For a swift moment their eyes met. "He is the last," the guardsman said and rode away.

The soldiers pushed Loma into the quiet group of children. They turned to look at him. Some of his friends smiled. Others were too afraid. Loma stared at them. Only their faces looked Hopi. A few had short haircuts, others had no haircuts at all. Most of the boys were dressed in work clothes. Two girls wore Spanish type dresses. But it wasn't the clothes that made them strange, it was the look in their eyes. Only a few months ago they had laughed and run and played together. They had sung songs, performed in ceremonies, lived in harmony. Now they stood bunched close together, guarded by Spanish soldiers, waiting to witness something they had no wish to see.

At the edge of the cramped group was Wickvaya and his young wife, who refused to lift her eyes to anyone. Wickvaya stood by her side, restless and unsure. In place of the kindness Loma had always seen in the dark eyes, was a hooded anger. The warmth drained from Loma's body. He stood and waited. The children waited. The people milled and talked.

"They are bringing out the prisoners!" a voice from the crowd shouted.

The people quickly separated and ran to the edge of the street, clearing the plaza for the prisoners. The talking voices settled into a hushed silence. From the jail came the prisoners being driven into the plaza by guardsmen on horses.

Loma could hardly believe the sight before him. Some of the prisoners had iron balls with sharp spikes tied to their feet. At the same time each was forced to throw a heavy iron ball with spikes over his shoulder, the spikes digging into his back at every throw. While the guardsmen drove the ball-and-spike prisoners around the plaza, other prisoners were tied to poles. Their arms were stretched over the poles, then each man was given hard lashes across the back.

The Hopi children stood, their eyes fixed, unbelieving. Loma recognized the young soldier who had taken him on the back of his horse, taught him Spanish words and let him keep his feet warm beneath his own legs. He wanted to cry out, to tell the governor that this man was not all bad. He lunged forward and was brought up sharply by a guardsman standing nearby.

Finally the iron balls were removed from the prisoners' legs, and the others were taken down from the heavy poles. Ropes were tied around each of them and they were hitched to wild horses, nervous with fear. When each prisoner was tied, the horses were turned loose and driven out of the plaza into the hills.

Loma could not look. He buried his head in his hands. The guardsman jerked the boy's hands away from his face. "Look!" he demanded. "You must watch so you can tell your people how the wicked soldiers were punished for their crime against your village!"

The guardsman spoke in rapid Spanish. Loma did not understand. He turned his head away from the guard and closed his eyes.

When the wild horses were out of sight, the crowd slowly dispersed. There was no laughter, no talking, only a group of depressed onlookers who walked away in the dust.

As the children were taken to the jailhouse where they would spend their last night in Santa Fe before being escorted to their homes the next day, Loma looked around for Big Jim and Josie and Beaver Charlie. He heard Big Jim's voice. He strained his eyes to see him.

Finally the three friends came into view. They walked by his side to the jailhouse. No one spoke, the heaviness of the moment was too great. On the steps of the jail, Big Jim reached out to Loma and drew him aside. A guardsman stepped swiftly between them.

Big Jim stood up towering over the guard. He had control of his words, but in his eyes there was fire. "You going to shoot me for talking to my boy?" Big Jim said.

The guardsman started to speak, stared up into the angry eyes of Big Jim, then stepped back, his hand grasping Loma's shoulder.

"Take your hands off him," Big Jim said evenly.

The guardsman withdrew his hand and placed it on his gun, ready in case the big mountain man started something.

Big Jim knelt in front of Loma. "This ain't goodbye, boy. Josie, Charlie and me will be here at sunrise to see you off. Charlie went back to the house and got this for you. The floor of a jail is mighty cold." He shoved the buffalo robe at Loma. The boy's solemn eyes made Big Jim look away. The man reached into his buckskin shirt and drew out a brown sack. "This here is enough candy to feed a whole tribe. You and the kids enjoy it tonight."

"Thank you," was all Loma could say.

"Oh, it ain't from me. Josie's the one. I'll give your thanks to her. Remember now, we'll see you in the morning." He stood up and faced the guard. "If I hear that the boy didn't get to use the buffalo robe and share the candy around with the kids, your scalp won't be worth the selling. Understand?"

Anger flashed in the guard's eyes. He understood.

"All right. See that you don't forget." Big Jim ruffled his hand awkwardly through Loma's black hair, then turned and quickly walked away.

Loma hugged the buffalo robe and the sack of candy closely to him as he went up the steps into the jail.

The next morning dark rain clouds hung over-head. The Spanish soldiers complained about the weather and the long ride ahead of them to Oraibi. They were satisfied that the governor had ordered the Hopi children home, but their satisfaction dwindled when he also ordered a detachment of soldiers to escort the group all the way back across the desert to Oraibi.

The horses were saddled and waiting in front of the jail-house when the children were ushered out. Loma looked around and found Big Jim, Josie and Beaver Charlie waiting for him. Holding the buffalo robe, he broke out of the group and ran to them. Big Jim caught the boy up in his arms, swung him around and set him down again. Loma stood before the group, not knowing what to say.

Josie broke the silence. "You will be home in time for Niman Kachina ceremony," she said.

Loma nodded.

"Yep," joined in Beaver Charlie. "Niman Kachina is a powerful important ceremony. It's the harvesting of winter prayers and planning. It's the time when the kachina spirits return to the lower world for the balance of the year, ain't it?"

Loma stared. "You know about Niman Kachina?"

"Paati told me some. See if I remember right." He cleared his throat. "Since the Winter Solstice the kachinas have been on this here earth to help the people with the Creation pattern for the year. How's that?"

"Good." Loma smiled.

Charlie grinned. "You see, I ain't so dumb after all. Let's see, now's the time when life is in full bloom. The first crops are coming in, so the kachinas' work is pretty much done. Since their work is finished here, they go to the lower world to help out there."

"And," said Josie, "it is the time when prayerful messages are sent on the wings of eagles to other planets and stars where there is life. In return we must have good thoughts to keep our own world in order. It is this that helps to keep harmony between man and nature."

Big Jim was bursting to say something. He tried to keep his voice calm. "Well," he said casually, "if it's so all-fired important I guess we'll have to watch it together." A big grin spread over his ruddy face.

Loma's eyes flew wide open. He stared at Big Jim. "You . . . you will be there?"

"Yep."

Tears of joy welled up in Loma's eyes. He swallowed hard.

Big Jim cleared his throat. "You see, today Josie and me are getting hitched the white man's way. Tomorrow we head out for her pueblo where we'll be tied by her people. That'll take a couple of weeks. They like to make a man suffer. Soon as we're married there, Charlie will catch up to us with the buckboard full of goods and the three us will head out for Oraibi."

Loma looked from Big Jim to Josie to Beaver Charlie. A bashful smile spread over his lips.

But Big Jim wasn't finished. "Maybe next winter," he said, "your folks will let you help me out."

Loma raised his face to Big Jim. Slowly, he shook his head.

"Why not?" Big Jim asked surprised.

"Killing beaver is not the Hopi way." he said softly.

"You're telling me!" Big Jim boomed. "But who said anything about trapping beaver?" His eyes sparkled with good humor.

"It is your way," Loma replied.

"Was!" Big Jim thundered. "I decided there are already too many beaver trappers. Why before you know it the streams and rivers won't have a beaver left. It ain't right. Beavers do a lot of good. I convinced Charlie that he's too doggone old to be trading around the country by himself. Be better to set up a trading post somewhere and let him run it while a younger man does the dirty work. He's a stubborn fool, can't see the right of something when it's under his nose. But I convinced him. I sure did."

Loma opened his mouth. Charlie winked. He closed it. Finally he said, "You will be a good partner to Beaver Charlie."

"That's telling him," Big Jim slapped Charlie on the back. "Well, Loma, what do you say? Be willing to spend some time with an old friend?"

Loma extended his hand, white man's style. Big Jim grasped it warmly.

"We will wait no longer!" a Spanish soldier called to Loma.

Josie hugged him. Loma handed the buffalo robe to Big Jim. "He meant you to keep it," Charlie said. Big Jim nodded.

They stood mute, wanting to say goodbye, but not saying anything. Beaver Charlie slapped Loma on the seat of his buckskin trousers. "Tell your ma to have plenty of piki bread. We're liable to be mighty hungry."

Loma nodded without looking up, turned and followed the soldier to the waiting group. He tied the buffalo robe behind the saddle, climbed up on the horse and slowly raised his hand to them. Once out of town he looked back and could see them standing, the size of dots, waiting while he rode out of sight.

High overhead the great clouds opened and the rain came, washing the dust out of the air and settling the loose dirt beneath the horse's hoofs. It was a steady rain that showed no signs of letting up. The children sat huddled over the horses' withers, uncomplaining. Loma sat still, head low, and studied his hands upon the reins. Wickvaya rode beside his young wife, saying nothing but looking at her from time to time.

By night the rain turned into a steady drizzle. Loma and the other children who had no blankets slept close together underneath the warm buffalo robe.

By morning the rain had done its work. The land was fresh and the children smiled. The rising sun sent its golden light over the big land, searching out the shadows, touching the wet, glistening rocks. The children rode closer together now, no longer feeling like strangers to each other. Sometimes they talked of home and how happy they were to be going back. No one spoke of the experiences of the past months. The punishment of the soldiers had opened the wound in their hearts. Until it healed, they would not speak of their time in slavery.

138

Loma's body warmed with light from the sun. There was magic in the air. He could feel it. All day he drank in the warmth of spring, slowly and with satisfaction. He recalled the cold and the fear of the trip months ago to Santa Fe. Now he and the others were crossing the same land eagerly.

At night Wickvaya told the children of their parents and the village. He told them of the tears and prayers that had followed them across the big land. And the children were glad that soon they would be home to comfort their parents, to help wash the bitterness away.

Each day the children's anticipation grew. They sat straight and still in the saddles, their eyes on the vast desert they knew and loved. The desert was a part of them, the sandstone cliffs, the sandy washes and scarred arroyos. They knew stories about the wind-twisted juniper trees, stubborn enough to grow out of rocks, brave enough to stay alive with little water.

Loma could not look enough at the desert around him. In the desert was a mystery of strength and silence, fire and peace. There was always the sand and sometimes the wind blew the sand, destroying crops, uprooting plants and making deep scars on the face of the earth. Loma thought about it and remembered how his father had taught him to work in harmony with the sand by using it for good and putting the bad away. His father had said that their ancestors first started using the sand dunes to plant corn and beans and squash. The plants kept the rain from washing the sand away and in that way the dunes were used to store water.

The children made a game of pointing out wild plants that their parents used in everyday life. They found plants used for medicines and chewing gum and food seasoning. The child who remembered the most names won the game, but in their joy they forgot to keep score and named the plants just for the fun of it. They found wild onions and the bitter tasting wild potato that they had often tasted mixed in mutton stew. The girls discovered plants used for dyes in basket weaving. The boys looked for the sweet cactus fruit eaten as candy.

When the group neared First Mesa they passed small flocks of sheep and watched the new lambs scamper in and out of the flock. Loma wondered if the people of his village had any sheep left after the Spanish soldiers had run them off.

The sun was low in the western sky when Loma first saw the outline of Third Mesa. Its slanted light flowed and tipped the mesa top with purple shadows. It smiled down upon his people, blessing them with a beautiful sunset.

The children and soldiers rode in the dusk and then in the night across the painted desert to Oraibi. Loma could smell juniper smoke as it drifted lazily from the high village houses to the big land below.

It was nearly midnight when the group reached the bottom of Third Mesa. The soldiers dismounted, gathered the horses together and made camp. Their job was over. They were tired and wished to be left alone.

Loma removed the buffalo robe from the back of the saddle and with Wickvaya, his young wife and the other children, began to climb up the footpath to the mesa top. His heart beat wildly as he followed the well-worn path upward. Once on top of the mesa, Loma looked back over the land they had crossed. The moon shed its light on the desert that stretched away on every side, spotted here and there by strong juniper trees twisted by the winds. The boy licked his dry lips and breathed deeply. He was home. This was where he belonged.

His eyes blinked, blurring the stare. He turned toward the village. The other children had gone on before him. He was alone. Gathering the buffalo robe tightly to him, he ran down the dusty street to his house.

He stood in front of the door. Inside the house was dark. There was no sound save the breathing of his parents as they slept. He stepped lightly through the doorway and smelled the scent of juniper wood and mutton stew mixed with sweet, indescribable odors of his parents, the village and the people. Yes, this was home.

He called softly, "Mother. Father. I am back."

They sat up slowly, in unison, as if in a dream. They looked at each other, then they saw their son standing in the darkness before them. Without a word they scrambled up from the blankets and went to Loma. For a long time his mother held him close to her. His father stood apart watching. Loma went to him, leaned his head against the man's chest and felt the security of the strong arms about him.

His mother quickly made a fire in the fireplace to light the small room. Then she set the pot of stew over the flames.

"You are hungry. You are tired," she insisted. "You must eat and sleep. Are you well? Were you harmed? Tell us of the days and nights you have been away."

His father smiled. The woman needed to talk. She needed to know about her son. For him, having Loma home again was enough.

"First you must eat," she said shoving a bowl of stew in front of the boy.

He accepted the food willingly and sat cross-legged on the floor to eat. They waited quietly for him to finish. Suddenly Loma looked up from the bowl. He smiled at them. "I am glad to be home," he said.

"Only our flesh was separated. Your spirit blended with ours," said his father.

Loma nodded. What his father said was true. He set the bowl aside and looked steadily into his father's eyes. "I was afraid," he admitted.

The man smiled kindly. "We must experience many emotions along the road of life. In the ignorance of fear, the eyes, the ears, the nose, and the mouth do not function. Did you, my son, step beyond the outer senses of fear?"

Loma nodded. "In my dreams I saw the greater life. Then I was not afraid."

Loma's mother smiled gratefully. If her son had conquered even some part of fear, now he would understand peace. "They did not harm you?" she asked.

"No. The Spaniards sold us in Santa Fe. I was bought by a white man called Big Jim."

"He was a good man?"

"Yes. I learned much from him and others." Loma told of his adventures until his eyes grew heavy and his father interrupted.

"It is almost time for the sun to make a new day. You sleep. We will hear the rest when you awaken."

Loma nodded and curled up on the blankets that his mother had fixed for him. He half-opened one eye. "Did I tell you," he mumbled sleepily, "that Big Jim and Josie and Beaver Charlie will be here for Niman Kachina ceremo . . .?" His voice trailed off. He was asleep.

The parents looked at each other. That made the fourth time Loma had told them. The woman smiled. "He will not be happy until I have ground a storeroom full of cornmeal for Beaver Charlie's piki bread."

Together the mother and father walked out of the house toward the rising sun in the east. They held cornmeal to their mouths, then the man raised his hands and the strength of his whispered words vibrated through the desert.

"Through all truths runs the one great truth; the spiritual oneness of all life. It is my son's chosen duty to walk the road of brotherhood. Guide him well that he may live in accordance with the pure pattern of Creation."

A NOTE ON THE
HISTORICAL BACKGROUND

Over one hundred years before the Southwest was divided
into states, the land was known as the territory of New Spain
and later the territory of New Mexico. The Spaniards ruled
the land, which included the villages of the Pueblo Indians
and the Hopi mesas, but they could not rule their religion.
Every time the Spaniards tried to force Christianity on the
Pueblo Indians, especially the Hopi, the people rebelled. The
Pueblo were a peaceful people and finally left to tend their
small farms and participate in their own religious ceremonies.

The Navajo Indians were a seminomadic tribe that
moved into the territory from the north. The Navajo came
into the land on foot, but soon discovered that with horses
they could move more swiftly. They raided the Spaniards'
livestock. From 1823 to 1832 companies of mounted
Spaniards pursued bands of marauding Navajo. The captured Navajo were taken to Santa Fe and sold as slaves.

But in 1832 a small company of Spanish soldiers invaded
the Hopi village of Oraibi on Third Mesa. The soldiers killed

several Hopi men and captured fourteen children and the young wife of Wickvaya, a Hopi youth. The Spaniards drove off the Hopi sheep and, with their captives, rode back to Santa Fe where the children were sold as slaves.[1]

Wickvaya was determined to get his wife back, so he set off on foot, alone. With the help of interpreters, he was admitted to the governor's palace in Santa Fe. After hearing that the captured children were Hopi, the governor issued an order to return all the children and the young wife of Wickvaya.

Before they left Santa Fe, all of the captured children were taken to witness the punishment meted out to their captors, then they were escorted home to Oraibi.

About this same time in history, white men who were not Spanish appeared on the scene. They were beaver trappers and known as mountain men. They dressed in buckskin, wore Indian moccasins, carried a rifle and a knife. At night they slept in a bearskin or buffalo robe.[2]

It is said that two famous mountain men, Old Bill Williams and, later, Joe Meek, passed through the Hopi villages. Old Bill Williams may have stayed there for a time.[3] They were followed by many others.

The first traders appeared in the mid-1830s in covered wagons, on mule back, and in open buckboards. In those years traders usually traveled from one place to another among the Indians. Later, the first permanent trading post was established near First Mesa for Hopi and Navajo alike.

[1]Waters, Frank. *Book of the Hopi.* New York: The Viking Press, 1963, pp. 268-269.
[2]Waters, Frank. *Masked Gods.* Denver: Sage Books, 1950, p. 57.
[3]Waters, *Book of the Hopi,* p. 270.

GLOSSARY

arroyo—A deep, dry gully or creek.

Bear clan—A leading Hopi clan.

kachina—Spirit of the invisible forces of life.

kachina doll—Small, painted wooden doll (usually from cotton-wood tree).

kachina mask—Masks worn by men in ceremonies. Each mask represents a spirit force.

kiva—Underground ceremonial chamber.

mesa—A high, broad and flat tableland with sharp, rocky cliffs descending to the surrounding desert.

Niman Kachina ceremony—"Home Dance." The going home of the kachinas. During the winter the kachinas come to the earth to help establish the Creation pattern for the year. In the spring, when their work is done, they go back to the "Lower World."

Oraibi Village—The oldest continuously inhabited settlement in the United States.

prayer stick—Called *páho* by the Hopi. There are simple and complex páhos. A simple one is a single willow stick to which is attached by means of a string of native cotton the down feather of an eagle. The stick represents the physical body; the string represents the life cord; and the feather, the loftiness of the spirit. Páhos are used to send messages to the Creator.

piki bread—Paper-thin wafer bread made from corn.

Powamu Society—Every Hopi child before reaching adolescence must be initiated into either the Kachina or Powamu societies.

Powamu ceremony—Purification of the life pattern for the whole year.

Sóyal—Symbolizes the second phase of Creation at the dawn of life.

Sóyal ceremony—Gives strength and direction to all budding life.

Taos—Small town in northern New Mexico.

travois—A sled constructed of a frame between two poles. The pole shafts are attached to either side of the horse.

FURTHER READING

Non-Fiction Books About the Hopi

Bassman, Theda. *Treasures of the Hopi*. Flagstaff: Northland Publishing, 1997.

Boissiere, Robert. *Meditations With the Hopi*. Rochester, Vt.: Inner Traditions International, Ltd., 1987.

Courlander, Harold. *The Fourth World of the Hopis: The Epic Story of the Hopi Indians As Preserved in Their Legends and Traditions*. Albuquerque: University of New Mexico Press, 1987.

———. *People of the Short Blue Corn: Tales and Legends of the Hopi Indians*. New York: Henry Holt & Co., 1996.

James, Harry C. *Pages from Hopi History*. Tucson: University of Arizona Press, 1974.

Lomatuway'Ma. *Hopi Ruin Legends: Kiqotutuwutsi*. Lincoln: University of Nebraska Press, 1993.

———. *Hopi Animal Tales*. Edited by Ekkehart Malotki. Lincoln: University of Nebraska Press, 1998.

Mails, Thomas E. *The Hopi Survival Kit*. New York: Penguin Books, 1997.

Qoyawayma, Polingaysi and Vada F. Carlson. *No Turning Back: A Hopi Indian Woman's Struggle to Live in Two Worlds.* Albuquerque: University of New Mexico Press, 1991.

Simmons, Leo W., Robert V. Hine. *Sun Chief: The Autobiography of a Hopi Indian.* New Haven: Yale University Press, 1972.

Waters, Frank. *Book of the Hopi.* New York: Viking Penguin, 1972.

Wilson, Terry P. *Hopi: Following the Path of Peace.* San Francisco: Chronicle Books, 1994.

Art Books

Blair, Mary Ellen and Laurence R. Blair. *The Legacy of a Master Potter: Nampeyo and Her Descendants.* Tucson: Treasure Chest Books, 1999.

Colton, Harold S. *Hopi Kachina Dolls.* Albuquerque: University of New Mexico Press, 1976.

Jacka, Jerry D. *Art of the Hopi: Contemporary Journeys on Ancient Pathways.* Flagstaff: Northland Publishing, 1998.

Kavena, Juanita Tiger. *Hopi Cookery.* Tucson: University of Arizona Press, 1980.

Picture Books

Kennard, Edward A. *Field Mouse Goes to War.* Las Cruces, Nm.: Kiva Publications, 2000.

Sage, Ana. *I Am Native American.* Designed by Erin McKenna. New York: The Rosen Publishing Group, Inc., 1998.

Schecter, Ellen. *The Warrior Maiden: A Hopi Legend.* Illus. by Laura Kelly. New York: Bantam Books, Inc., 1992.

Spence, Peggy D. Council of Indian Education. *The Day of the Ogre Kachinas: A Hopi Indian Fable.* Illus. by Jan H. Hammond. Niwot, Co.: Roberts Rinehart Publications, 1994.

Tomchek, Ann Heinrichs. *The Hopi.* New True Books. Oakland, Me.: Danbury Children's Press, 1994.

Middle Grade

Dewey, Jennifer Owings. *Rattlesnake Dance: True Tales, Mysteries, and Rattlesnake Ceremonies.* Honesdale, Pa.: Boyds Mills Press, 1997.

Hawk, Virginia Driving. *The Hopi: A First Americans Book.* New York: Holiday House, 1995.

Mana, Tawa, and Youyou Seyah. *When Hopi Children Were Bad: A Monster Story.* Siena Oaks Publishing Co., 1992.

Price, Joan. *Hawk in the Wind.* New York: Royal Fireworks Press, 1998.

——. *Medicine Man.* New York: Royal Fireworks Press, 2000.

——. *Little Echo.* New York: Royal Fireworks Press, 2001.

Sears, Bryan P., and G. S. Prentzas. *The Hopi Indians.* Junior Library of American Indians. Broomall, Pa.: Chelsea House Publishing, 1994.

Smith, Roland. *The Last Lobo.* New York: Disney Press, 1999.

Young Adult

MacGregor, Rob. *Prophecy Rock.* New York: Bantam Doubleday Dell Books for Young Readers, 1998.

Vick, Helen Hughes. *Walker of Time.* Niwot, Co.: Roberts Rinehart, 1993.

——. *Walker's Journey Home.* Niwot, Co.: Roberts Rinehart, 1995.

——. *Tag Against Time.* Niwot, Co.: Roberts Rinehart, 1996.